BRIDES:
From Blushing
to Bawling
(And Everything
In Between)

On Newsstands Now:

TRUE STORY
and
TRUE CONFESSIONS
Magazines

True Story and *True Confessions* are the world's largest and best-selling women's romance magazines. They offer true-to-life stories to which women can relate.

Since 1919, the iconic *True Story* has been an extraordinary publication. The magazine gets its inspiration from the hearts and minds of women, and touches on those things in life that a woman holds close to her heart, like love, loss, family and friendship.

True Confessions, a cherished classic first published in 1922, looks into women's souls and reveals their deepest secrets.

To subscribe, please visit our website:
www.TrueRenditionsLLC.com or call **(212) 922-9244**

To find the TRUES at your local store, please visit:
www.WheresMyMagazine.com

BRIDES:
From Blushing to Bawling
(And Everything
In Between)

From the Editors
Of *True Story* And
True Confessions

Published by True Renditions, LLC

True Renditions, LLC
105 E. 34th Street, Suite 141
New York, NY 10016

ISBN: 978-1-938877-89-6

Visit us on the web at www.truerenditionsllc.com.

Contents

THE AWFUL, HORRIBLE, EVERYTHING-WENT-WRONG WEDDING

Just when I thought Mom would ruin my big day,
once and for all—she turned around and
made it a memory to treasure always!

"This is a disaster!" my mother declared. "Winnie, you might as well call it off!"

"Doris!" my best friend, Kimber, cried at my mother, shocked. "What are you saying?"

"I'm saying that this is not the wedding she dreamed of. Between those horrible . . . people of Ashton's and all our bad luck, I think she should announce that she's changed her mind. It's the only way out of this awful mess. At least then, we can leave the church with our heads held high!"

I took a deep breath.

"Winnie?" my mother asked again, her voice sharp and shrill.

Ever since I was five years old, Mom and I had been talking about my wedding. My mother didn't have a wedding; she and my father got married at City Hall. Sometimes I think she thinks that's why Dad vamoosed when I was two. Maybe she thinks a big church wedding would've made it all different. Anyway, she and I would talk about it all the time. It was our big thing. We had a scrapbook full of pictures ripped out of bridal magazines of gowns and cakes and different kinds of bows for the pews—no kidding. My mother—somewhere, somehow—had learned a lot about weddings and she knew that the bride's family traditionally paid for everything, so early on, she'd started The Wedding Fund. She'd put a couple of dollars in it after grocery shopping, I'd put in the fifty cents I'd gotten from taking cans back to the recycling center. I don't think either of us was really aware of how much a wedding actually costs, but the fund did grow.

Growing up, I had a few girlfriends who were just as obsessed, though as we got older, it got a little embarrassing. I remember one of my girlfriends looking at my scrapbook and saying, "Have you given any thought to the actual guy, Winnie? Or are you just interested in the wedding?"

Well, I thought that was kind of sarcastic. And I didn't see any harm in it, though it certainly wasn't something I showed any of my high school boyfriends. They would've run out the door at the very mention of that scrapbook, leaving one of those cartoon outlines behind them!

In fact, the scrapbook had been relegated to the top shelf of my closet sometime during high school. And it hadn't been brought out since.

Mom worked as an office manager and after high school, I got a job working in the same huge building that she worked in, on a different floor, working for a group of architects. I liked the work, but it wasn't long before I realized that my social life had come to a screeching halt after high school. Most of the old crowd I'd hung out with had paired off or gone on to college or into the military. And most of the people I worked with were married or engaged or otherwise settled down.

Of course, a few dates came my way. But even before the second date, Mom always had a lot of opinions. They were too sloppy in their dress; they drove a car that needed work. I would kid her that there weren't that many perfect guys running around out there, but the funny thing is, the minute she pointed out all of their faults, I'd start seeing them, too, and any idea of romance would be out the window. Most Saturday nights, I stayed home with my mother, criticizing what little there was on TV.

So the years slid by.

I moved up a couple of notches at the office and by the time I was twenty-five, I was sort of the office manager myself, though there were only two other secretaries for me to "reign" over.

I hadn't been on a date in over six months. I was actually beginning to wonder if there was something seriously wrong with me when I met Ashton. He was a computer systems guy, and when we got a new computer system at the firm, he came in to set it up and work out all the bugs. He ended up staying on at the firm for about a month, and by the end of that time, my coworkers were joking that he was thinking up new things to go wrong with the system just so he could stay and flirt with me.

For a long time, I didn't think that Ashton was serious about me. He's a fun guy, always something going on. Our first date was at a karaoke bar, and Ashton was the life of the party. After that, we went to an amusement park, and then whitewater rafting on a river about fifty miles away. We always did a lot of laughing, but there was time for talk, too. Six months after our first date, he asked me to marry him. I was dumbfounded. Even though I knew I was falling in love, I'd had no clue that Ashton felt the same way.

"Winnie, we fit together like two pieces of a puzzle," he said.

I felt the same way. I had been pretty popular in school and I'd

2

gone out with a lot of guys and none of them had ever made me feel comfortable the way Ashton did. I felt I could be completely myself with him; there was no need for pretenses whatsoever. And I could see a future with Ashton that I hadn't been able to imagine with anyone else. So I said yes to his proposal.

Mom, of course, had the usual criticisms about Ashton: His hair was too long, he dressed too sloppily, he didn't have a serious demeanor, and he laughed too much. However, in Ashton's case, it was like all of those criticisms just slid off of me like water off a duck's back; they didn't bother me for an instant. Ashton was funny. He made me laugh. And whenever I was with him, it was like the whole world opened up to me and possibilities that I hadn't even guessed at presented themselves.

Ashton comes from a big family, and of course, my family is just Mom and I. I met all of the Farmers at a picnic early on in our courtship. I remember thinking how overwhelming they all were. Ashton has four brothers and a sister, and there was a whole lot of shouting and arguing (Ashton said it was just discussing) and laughter. After I'd been with them for about an hour or so, though, my unease simply melted away. The Farmer family ran an auction house and everyone had some job there, and whenever they had time off, they all got together (like they didn't work with each other almost every single day) and blew off steam.

Predictably, my mother didn't like any of them. Shortly after Ashton and I got engaged, Mom and I were invited to Ashton's parents' house for dinner. Needless to say, the evening was a little chaotic. Ashton is the youngest boy and all the others—except his sister—are married and they have kids and seem to live right around the corner from their parents.

That night, the whole brood was in attendance—from howling babies to sullen teenagers—and there was lots of talking and joking about the wedding. My mother sat stiffly through it all, and then in the car on the way home, all she could talk about was how overweight Vicki (Ashton's mother) was, and how untidy their house was.

"Well, sure, Mom," I said. "But we have just the two of us to clean up after."

That didn't cut the mustard with my mother. As you can probably imagine, she's tidy and well organized and I can see, in retrospect, how Ashton's parents' house must've been overwhelming for her, just like it was for me, at first.

However, I'd have to say that the Farmers definitely didn't grow on her like they did on me. Ashton's father even had a cute brother, Uncle Clint, who took a shine to my mother at one of the Farmers' subsequent get-togethers. Mom kind of thought he'd call her. When he didn't, I asked Ashton what had happened.

He hedged for a while, but then he finally said, "Look, sweetie, Uncle Clint really thinks your mom is good looking and all that. But he says she takes herself too seriously. I guess she didn't laugh at his jokes or something."

It was no big deal, but I began to realize that my mother didn't laugh very much at anything. Or smile, for that matter. She was just a serious, down-to-business kind of person.

As the wedding neared, the scrapbook came out. Some of the ideas in it didn't seem so dreamy to me anymore, now that I was twenty-five instead of fourteen. For instance, I had to talk my mother out of ice sculptures; I didn't want my wedding reception to be mistaken for an all-you-can-eat cruise ship buffet! And embossed napkins seemed like a little too much, too.

"And after all, Mom—I know that The Wedding Fund isn't all that big," I said.

"Oh, it has enough in it," she said vaguely, so that I realized that she'd taken out some kind of ridiculous loan. I wasn't going to say that she couldn't do it, because I knew that would be pointless, but it became my policy to try to pull off the wedding without it being too expensive.

Ashton's mom, Vicki, was a great coconspirator. After all, she'd raised a huge family on the profits from the auction company, and while the Farmers were earning a living, it wasn't an extraordinary living, by any means.

In one of our first conversations on the subject, she asked me if we could have the wedding at the neighborhood church that all the Farmers went to. "That way, the church ladies will all come to the reception and bring a dish to pass," she said. From this starting point, we worked out how someone would make the cake for not a lot of money, and how someone else would devise some sort of punch and find a great, big punchbowl somewhere.

My mother was outraged. She wanted me to be married in the cathedral downtown.

"Mom, we aren't even Catholic."

"So? Maybe they rent it out."

"I don't think so. The Farmers' church will be fine, Mom. As it is, we've still got to find my dress and the decorations for the church, pick the attendants, and all that."

Of course, we fought over the dress. But at least I won that battle. I wanted something long and slinky in ivory silk that I could conceivably wear somewhere else, if we were ever invited someplace swanky. Mom had her mind set on something long and lacy and incredibly expensive. But I found what I wanted on a remainder rack at Helgenberger's.

4

"Winnie, but we've both been dreaming about this for years," Mom whispered pleadingly.

In that moment, I realized that I hadn't actually been thinking about my wedding much since the scrapbook had gone up onto the closet shelf. I was much more interested, right at that moment, in the two weeks we were both taking off from our jobs to go on a honeymoon cruise and tour of Alaska, and in the small house we were buying that was all ready for us to move in. I was much more concerned with starting my married life and eventually, starting a family. My mother, however, seemed stuck at the wedding. I was beginning to wish that she'd had a wedding of her own so she could let me have mine.

I finally relented and let her spend a god-awful amount on the flowers, which made her happy, and they were, indeed, gloriously beautiful. I'd also had a little talk with Ashton and we'd decided that the flowers that decorated the church and reception would be taken later to a local children's ward so all that beauty wouldn't be wasted. Except my bouquet, of course, which was a work of art in ivory and pink roses.

Ashton had an uncle named Peter, and I noticed that he was turning up at a lot of family dinners and sitting next to my mother. She refused to acknowledge her interest to me, but I noticed that her outfits were getting more and more elaborate, which was a sign. It was a little silly, really—she'd arrive for backyard barbeques looking like something out of a nineteenth-century lawn party with a big hat and wide skirt. Uncle Peter seemed to like her sense of style, but in the weeks before the wedding, when I would've expected him to ask her out, he didn't. So I finally asked Ashton about it.

"Oh, he likes her," he told me one night as we were busy writing out guest names on little placards for the reception. (Yes, you guessed it—my mother's idea.) "The whole family's twittering about it, actually; he hasn't really shown an interest in anyone since Aunt Carol died. And that was five years ago."

"So why doesn't he ask her out, then?"

"The truth, Winnie?"

I whacked him playfully. "I thought there were to be no secrets between us."

"Well, I think he does like her. But he asked me yesterday: Does she ever laugh? Does she get his jokes? Does she ever even smile?"

Well, it wasn't something I'd asked myself about my mother very often. She was just . . . my mother. But that night, when she was long asleep, I went through some old photos, taken when I was only a baby and my father was still with us. Mom did a lot of smiling in those pictures. There were several of the three of us, and she was positively beaming. In one, she was even laughing, looking up at my father like he was good enough to eat.

I lay in bed, trying to imagine how I would feel if, when our baby was only a couple of years old, Ashton vanished one night with no explanation beyond a drained checking account. And never came back, never phoned. I didn't know if I'd be able to be as strong as my mother was. But I also didn't know how to tell her that it was okay to laugh again, okay to enjoy life again. As it was, the only thing she seemed to truly enjoy was making my wedding more formal, complicated, and lacy.

Vicki, at least, had helped me economize on a couple of things, including the cake, which was being baked by one of the legions of "church ladies" at a greatly reduced price because it was being done for Vicki. My mother and I spent hours and hours fashioning these elaborate, ivory-and-emerald bows with trailing ribbons for the ends of each pew in the church. Ashton's niece, Daisy, would be our flower girl, and her twin brother, Damian, would be our ring bearer.

I would have to say, looking back, that everything went reasonably well—

Until the morning of the wedding.

I don't remember exactly who decided that we'd have an evening wedding. My mother thought it would be elegant, and there was an earlier wedding scheduled at the church that day. Our plane tickets were for early the next morning, so it all seemed to work out fine, initially.

But when I woke up that morning, it was gray and threatening out, and my mother was on her—what—sixteenth cup of coffee and buzzing around the kitchen like an out-of-sorts bee.

"It's going to rain," she said the moment I walked into the kitchen.

"It'll be fine, Mom."

"The pictures will all be dark."

"Mom, you wanted an evening wedding; of course they'll be dark."

"But I thought we could take pictures before—"

"It'll be okay, Mom, calm down."

It was like telling a hurricane to slow down and go the other way.

My friend, Kimber, was coming over at ten so we could get started on our beauty regimen—which would mostly be just the two of us having fun together—for the day, and my mother had a beauty parlor appointment at ten-thirty. By the time Kimber arrived, Mom had gone and—with any luck—would be gone for hours.

"I love her dearly, but she drives me crazy," I confessed to Kimber.

She laughed. "Imagine how she'll be when you have a baby!"

"I don't think it'll be the same. Now the baby's wedding—that'll be another story!"

"So maybe your mom should have a wedding of her own."

I thought of Ashton's Uncle Peter. "I think she's going to have to unclench a little or that's never going to happen."

We did each other's nails and then she put some subtle highlights in my hair. We talked about a million things, the way girls do, and before we knew it, it was almost six and time to go to the church, where I'd put on my gown. The wedding was to begin promptly at eight.

Kimber and I hadn't been paying much attention to the weather all that day, but it was really pouring when we left for the church. Mom had gone ahead an hour earlier to put all of those bows on the end of the pews.

When we got to the church and walked into the room where the brides get ready, she was literally wringing her hands. "No one's going to come!" she wailed. "This wedding is going to be a disaster!"

In the next hour, we did get several calls from out-of-town relatives and friends who said they weren't coming. It was a big storm system, going across several states. A serious thunderstorm was expected later that night.

"It'll be fine," I kept saying.

"And the cake looks like someone drunk made it!" Mom wailed on her eighth trip into my dressing room.

Things didn't get really hairy, however, until Vicki poked her head in around seven. "We've got some leaks in the roof," she announced.

"Oh, dear God," my mother moaned.

"We're putting some pans and buckets out. Looks like we should've re-roofed last spring."

By this point, my mother's perfectly coiffed hair was beginning to frizz from all her dashing about. In the last hour in the dressing room, it got a little hectic as several of Ashton's sisters-in-law were in there with me, along with their children, and Daisy and Damian. My mother kept trying to shoo them all out, but they kept coming in the other way.

Finally, though, Kimber and I were dressed. She was looking very fetching in her emerald-green dress, and we beamed at each other. Then she got my veil and carefully arranged it on my head.

At that moment, one of the more rollicking young nephews, evidently in the midst of playing hide-and-seek, whipped around me carrying a purloined cup of punch. Both Kimber and I saw it coming, and we both moved to stop it, but that cup of punch seemed to have a devilish life of its own, and it sloshed and spilled, landing all over the bodice and skirt of my gown. Of course—

The punch was red.

Immediately, Mom shooed everyone out of the room, and I could hear them all thronging into the church, whispering about how, "The bride's dress is ruined! David did it! The bride's dress is ruined!"

That's when Mom made her dramatic pronouncement.

"What do you mean?" I asked her. "Just walk out?"

She nodded emphatically. "The storm of the century is raging outside, the roof is leaking, the cake is lopsided, and your dress is completely ruined!"

I took a very deep breath. I knew how much my wedding meant to my mother, and part of me had always wanted to give her that joy and satisfaction. But another part of me—apparently, the stronger part—had more sense.

I thought of our quiet life together—always just the two of us, eating dinner together, sharing a few anecdotes from our respective days. Watching television later, cultivating a few favorites that we enjoyed. Mom was a cross-stitcher, and I had gotten into crocheting. Then, next morning, we'd be back at work. Yes, our life together had definitely had a certain serenity to it.

But then I thought about Ashton's clan. Serene, they were not. In fact, if they were anything, the Farmers were actually a little too full of life. Mom and I could probably teach them a thing or two about good organization, but, then—they could probably teach us a thing or two about living life to its fullest.

Vicki stuck her head in the door. "I heard there was trouble," she said. "And I've gotta say—the leaks aren't getting any better, either. We'd better go now."

"Honey?" Mom said to me, clearly expecting me to say something to Vicki.

I took a deep breath. Outside, thunder growled ominously. "I'm ready," I said.

Vicki winked at me as if she'd read my mind. "Good girl," she said. "I'll alert the troops."

"I'll get something to wipe off your dress," Kimber said, scurrying into the bathroom.

"It won't help," my mother said dourly.

"Mom," I said, turning to her quietly, "we're going through with this, right now. It's going to be a beautiful wedding."

"But it's spoiled!"

"We love each other, Mom. It'll be beautiful."

I could tell she didn't believe a word I was saying, but she gave a little nod.

Kimber came back and dabbed at my dress with a wet paper towel, but truthfully, there wasn't much that could be done about the stain. "Maybe you can dye it black or something," Kimber suggested, grinning up at me from where she knelt on the floor. "That would be sexy."

"Luckily, I have a big bouquet. I'll use it to hide the stain."

"There's nothing funny about this," Mom pronounced.

Kimber had never stood up to my mother that I could recall. Who ever had, actually? But she did now.

"We're making the best of it, Mrs. Franklin," she said quietly, but firmly.

And then it was time to go.

Daisy and Damian preceded us down the aisle. Daisy threw rose petals and Damian waved excitedly to his relatives, which hadn't been part of Mom's plan. Then Kimber proceeded down the aisle, sidestepping a couple of big pans that had been placed here and there to collect the rainwater that dripped steadily from the cracked ceiling.

Then it was our turn.

For a moment, I thought, Maybe she's right. This is crazy. There was another crack of thunder and a stunning flash of lightning lighted up the windows of the church momentarily.

But then I caught sight of Ashton. He was waiting for me at the altar, laughing a little at our predicament, but beyond that, I saw a loyalty and steadfastness in his eyes—the very same qualities that had attracted me to him from our very first meeting.

I couldn't wait to get down that aisle and marry him before he got away.

"Who gives this woman?" the pastor asked when we'd reached the end of the aisle and had joined Ashton before the altar.

"I do," Mom said, in a tone that clearly said that she wished she had another few minutes to think about it.

I stepped up the two steps to the altar, where Ashton got his first good look at his lovely bride steeped in cherry punch. To the right of the pastor, a garbage can had been brought in to catch a really impressive stream of rainwater that poured steadily from the ceiling—sounding not unlike a babbling brook!

I don't know who started laughing first. Ashton and I always blame each other. And it was funny, this soggy ending to the perfect wedding. Ashton's brother, the best man, joined in, and Kimber, who I think thought the whole thing was funny from the very beginning, was only too happy to join in the merriment. Then Ashton's family caught the humor and the church was filled with good-natured laughter: Even the best-laid plans and all that.

I turned to my mother, who was standing in the first pew. To my horror, I could see that she was about to cry. I reached out to her—the wedding decorum was long gone—and we hugged.

"You wanted a memorable wedding, Mom," I whispered to her lovingly.

"But not like this!" she wailed.

9

Our eyes locked then, and at last, to my intense happiness, she finally got it: How it didn't matter if the bows were bedraggled, if my gown was spoiled. This was the start of my life with Ashton and I needed—and wanted—her with me. And if that was true, then everything else was icing on the cake.

And Mom started to laugh.

Then I returned to my place at the altar, with various members of Ashton's family patting my mother on the back.

"Dearly beloved," the pastor began—

And then there was another tremendous crash of thunder—and all the lights went out.

The Church Ladies were dispatched for matches and within a few minutes, they had the altar lit and little sconces around the church throwing light. And then (and this was the real miracle of the night) the rain actually let up for a few blessed minutes—long enough for us to say our vows in peace, in the romantic setting of candlelight.

For a moment then, it really was the wedding of my mother's dreams.

Luckily, the reception room was in the basement—and snug.

And, yes—the wedding cake was, in fact, lopsided. But it tasted pretty darn good! The band we'd hired wasn't great, but they were certainly energetic, and most everybody took a turn or two around the dance floor. Ashton and I left early; naturally, we had an agenda of our own. I threw my bouquet into the crowd and it sailed past all of my office friends and Ashton's pretty nieces—and straight into my mother's hands.

She blushed pink and laughed. And that's when I noticed that Uncle Peter was right there beside her to lead her into another dance.

"Maybe we shouldn't go right now," I said to Ashton. "I have to see how this ends!"

"We'll catch up with them in a couple of weeks," he said, grinning as he squeezed my hand lovingly. "Maybe by then, your mother will have designed her own perfect wedding."

I kissed him. "If she learned anything at all from this, she finally understands that it's really not all about the dress and the cake."

We kissed again and headed out to the waiting limousine. The last thing I heard was my mother laughing.

THE END

MY BACHELORETTE PARTY
RUINED MY WEDDING!

When Jenny told me that the girls I worked with at JumpStart Computers planned on throwing me a wild bachelorette party, my initial reaction was to wrinkle my face up as if I smelled something foul. I always hated bachelorette parties—the noise, the drinking, the stupid male strippers, and the naughty games.

That was the kind of reckless behavior you did when you're single and nothing matters, not when you have the man of your dreams committing his life to you. It all seemed so horribly immature that I wanted to back right out of it.

"You can't do that," Paul insisted as we cuddled on my sofa one evening. "You'll hurt their feelings. Anyway, it's tradition. It won't kill you to do something kind of crazy, Monica. No offense, but since we've been engaged and planning this wedding, you've been kind of stressed out. Grouchy I guess is the word. Maybe this will loosen things up a little and get you all frisky in time for our honeymoon."

I knew he was teasing, but it hit a sore spot. I'd been kind of difficult to be around since trying to pull together a huge June wedding with only three months to work with. I loved Paul with all of my heart, but he wasn't a planner. He didn't like to go with me when I went to talk with caterers, florists, deejays, and limo companies to book them for our big day. He said it was the bride's job to arrange all of that and he would simply pay for it.

It didn't make much sense, because my two older sisters were married and I remembered their fiancés getting involved in all the planning of the wedding. Chris even wanted to dance with my sister, Marti, when they interviewed each deejay to see which one felt right. Will insisted on samples of the different kinds of wedding cakes when he accompanied Carly to the caterers for their reception plans. I wanted to ask Paul where he got the notion that putting together a wedding was just the bride's responsibility, but I figured it didn't matter. These were small things compared to a lifetime of love.

"I'm still not interested in a dumb party," I scoffed, crossing my legs and bouncing my foot up and down. "Everybody gets together for a night of drinking and acting like idiots all in the honor of the most cherished day of my life. What kind of junk is that?"

He smiled and leaned toward me, tenderly kissing my cheek. "That's why I love you so much. You're a very deep-thinking girl. Just sometimes, I think you should loosen up and have fun."

11

"Like you're going to do for your party?" I asked, hating the thought of it, but knowing Tony and the guys were going to do it big. "Your brother and all your friends are probably going to have a harem of women and porno movies in honor of our upcoming nuptials."

"So?" Paul replied, as calm as could be. "What's wrong with that?"

My jaw went slack. This was the man who was going to sleep next to me for the rest of my life. Be my best friend. My soul mate. My lover forever. The future father of my children. Did he really think sex and booze was a good combination before two people exchange such serious vows?

I pulled away from him and began fussing with some loose threads on my forest green throw pillows. "It's like cheating," I muttered. "It feels dirty and wrong. I can't believe you think it's a good idea."

His laugh was deep and made me want to punch him. "How can it be like cheating when it's simply a harmless tradition? Cheating is something you do in secret hoping no one will find out. A bachelor or bachelorette party is something you enjoy with all of your friends and relatives. Everybody knows what you're doing. It's hardly the same thing."

"So, you can still ogle naked women when I'm not around and possibly touch and feel, but it's not cheating as long as your friends are there with you?"

"Exactly," he answered, contented I was finally getting the picture.

"And I can drool over chiseled naked men bumping and grinding in my face, possibly touching and getting carried away, but as long as the girls are around me, it's all okay by you."

"Yeah." He nodded, looking at me like I had some kind of third eye in the middle of my forehead. "What's the big deal? We'll be married after that and only have each other for the rest of our lives. What's one night?"

I shrugged, now pulling the threads on my throw pillow a little too hard and causing the seam to unravel. "I guess it's nothing," I answered, clenching my jaw. "If you think it's okay, then I guess I should, too. What's good for the goose—whatever that phrase is."

He smiled sensuously and pulled me up close to him. It normally felt wonderful to be in Paul's arms, but at the moment I was seeing him with a bevy of beauties wearing nothing but perfume and trying my darndest to feel it was just tradition. He sensed my tension and planted a long kiss on my mouth. It was impossible to stay rigid then. Ice has no chance at staying frozen when a blowtorch comes along.

"Tonight's the big night," Jenny gushed while dropping a manila folder on my desk. "I hope you're not working too hard so you have some energy left for your party. It's going to be wild."

I looked up from over the frames of my glasses. The dreaded day had come no matter how I willed it away, but since Paul had stated how "grouchy" he thought I had gotten since making wedding plans, I didn't dare complain about it anymore. My strategy was to just get through it and get it over with. I'd act like I was supposed to act and make everybody happy, but it still felt rotten. I had no interest in getting drunk and watching musclemen peeling off their clothes in my honor. In fact, I would've preferred a hot bath and a good book, but according to Paul, I needed to loosen up a bit.

"I'm good," I answered, papering on a smile. "I'm fine. Filled with energy. Never better."

Jenny paused and examined my expression. "Are you sure? Is something wrong?"

I squirmed, picking up the folder she brought, and absently flipping through it. Names of clients blurred together as I felt her curious gaze burning into me. "Just stressed. The wedding has been a big project and it will be nice to get everything over with and just settle down and enjoy married life in a couple of weeks."

She winked one of her overly made-up eyes. "I think tonight will do wonders for your stress. From what I hear about this place from Michelle, when she had her bachelorette bash, the strippers really know how to treat a woman. Maybe you'll even get a special massage."

Her giggle trailed behind her, along with a cloud of cheap perfume. I leaned back in my chair and let out a long sigh. The whole thing was as funny as a crutch. The temptation to bow out declaring food poisoning or a case of the hives toyed with my mind for the hundredth time. Then Paul called and made me actually determined to go.

"I just wanted to say have fun tonight," he said cheerfully. "After all, Monica, it's your last chance to be a wild woman before I make a boring housewife out of you."

His words zinged me like a bolt of lightning. Was that how he saw our plans for marriage? He was going to tie me down like a ball and chain, then transform me into some frump with nothing but a sponge mop for excitement?

"Oh, I'm going to be a wild woman, all right," I answered back. "You might even have to bail me out of jail by the time this party is done."

I wanted it to bug him. I longed for some kind of jealousy or insecurity in his voice. Instead, he sounded as pleased as ever. "That would be a howl. You'd look sexy in stripes. I'm just glad you're finally getting in to the spirit of this whole thing. You've always been too cautious and cool. It's time to live a little!"

Live a little? Was that what he wanted me to do in a room full of gorgeous, naked men? "I'll do that," I answered curtly. "In fact, I may even live a lot. How would that be?"

Again, he laughed as if he hadn't a care in the world. "Oh, my Monica is a tigress underneath that conservative exterior. I hope those guys are ready to take you on!"

Now I felt sick. My own fiancé, finding humor in the possibility of my having multiple sexual romps with a group of strippers while my engagement ring sparkles on my left hand. The girls in the office were all excited about drinking, watching the men peel off their clothes, and getting out of control. Even my two sisters, Marti and Carly, were looking forward to the festivities. Neither of them had a bachelorette party. Instead, they each had bridal showers and ended up with tons of toasters and housewares. Not a single nude man in sight. They were thrilled I was having a party like this and told me they wouldn't miss it for the world. Carly actually told me that she envied me for it. Her husband didn't approve of her having one when they were about to get married. Wow. A man with a jealous streak. How refreshing. What I wouldn't give for Paul to have one. Maybe we could have spent tonight together renting a favorite video and snuggling together on the couch instead of my having to be surrounded by naked studs.

The strip club was every bit as tacky as I expected it would be. Guys with skintight black pants, no shirts, and black bowties greeted us at the door. Their upper arms were bigger than my waist and their ab muscles looked like an old-fashioned scrub board covered in skin. My sisters cooed and laughed as the bulky guys opened the door for our group and let us all pass by. Unfortunately, the muscle at the front doors was nothing compared to what awaited us inside.

"Welcome, ladies. I'm Donnie. Who is the bride to be?" A lean, athletic guy appeared before us in nothing but a gold g-string. The girls went ballistic, some even reaching to touch his arm just to see if he was real. Most had husbands with potbellies and thinning hair and went into culture shock mode.

Jenny nudged me forward. "This is Monica. I hope you'll treat her right tonight."

In one sweeping motion, Donnie slung me over his bare shoulder and began carting me off in cavemen style. "She's going to get the treatment," he called back to the howling group. "In fact, we've got a special seat for her."

"Put me down!" I screamed. "What are you, insane?"

He kept walking, taking long easy strides, as if he was merely carrying a sack of potatoes. "The shy type, huh?" he said, spanking me on my fanny. "I knew my first night would be a challenge."

"First night?" I said, trying to look at his face from the awkward position I was in. "This is your first night? You don't even act nervous or embarrassed."

He came to a velveteen throne right up front by the stage and carefully set me down in it. There were long tables set up for the girls on the left and the right, but I was definitely secluded.

"You're the one who should be nervous." He grinned. "You're getting married."

I squirmed against the seat and quickly went to smooth my messed up hair. "What's so scary about that?"

He looked around the club with slanted eyes. "I can always walk if I don't like it here. You're going to be trapped for life."

It shouldn't have knocked me off balance like it did, but his comment was like salt in a wound. Instantly, tears welled in my eyes as I clenched my jaws together.

"Trapped is not how I view my life with Paul." I snorted. "He's a wonderful guy who loves me very much and would give me the world if he could."

"Really?" Donnie responded, smirking like he didn't believe me. "Then what are you doing here? If I had a special lady that I gave my heart to, you can bet she wouldn't be in a place like this. I'd keep her all to myself." He winked at me and walked away.

He hit the nail right on the head. That was exactly what had hurt me so much about how Paul reacted to this corny bachelorette party. He seemed to enjoy the fact that I would be with other men instead of wanting to cherish me for himself. It was tradition. Here, take my fiancé, strip for her, pour booze down her throat, and even get wild so she ends up in the slammer. She'd look sexy in stripes—yes, siree. Enjoy her while you can because soon she'll be a boring housewife. . . . I could even picture his face. His eyes would be dancing with delight over the whole thought of my being surrounded by sexy men. What I really wanted was to be loved like Donnie had said. Why didn't Paul feel like he did?

"The guys here are so hot," Carly called out from her seat at the table to my left. "That Donnie guy was a real knockout!"

Tara, our sixty-two-year-old office coordinator, widened her eyes and nodded. "I haven't drooled this much since I ran out of gas in front of the donut shop when I was on my grapefruit diet."

Waiters in black g-strings came and took everyone's orders for drinks. I was going to go for a diet soda, but everyone else had ordered beer or wine.

You're too cautious, Monica—live a little. Paul's voice echoed in my ears and didn't go away until I ordered a rum and cola.

The show was obnoxious. Chiseled men in firemen outfits, cop outfits, doctor outfits, and construction worker outfits paraded on

15

stage and proceeded to strip down to next to nothing, grinding their goods in the girls' faces before concentrating on me. I hated it. Even two rum and colas didn't loosen me up. I just closed my eyes and waited for it to be over. It actually got hard to breathe.

Intermission came and I bolted to the ladies' room. I was on drink number four and was feeling rather dizzy, but not even close to being drunk enough to enjoy myself. Before I got to the restroom, I passed the payphone where Donnie was in a heated conversation with someone. It wasn't any of my business, but I couldn't help slowing my step and overhearing. It amazed me to learn he was talking to his mother.

"I told you this is just temporary, Mom. I'm not going to let him evict you. I'll stay here long enough to make enough money to make sure you can hold on to your apartment, and then I can quit. I'll go back to school. I don't want you to get all upset over it."

My breath caught. So he wasn't the stripper type. This was a desperate attempt to keep a roof over his mother's head.

He continued to lean against the wall with his back to me. "Mom? What's wrong? You don't sound good. You're getting too worked up."

In a few seconds, he slammed the phone down and ripped the bow tie from his neck. It was then that he locked eyes with me and realized I had heard what just happened.

"Do you have a car here?" He seemed absolutely panic-stricken.

"Of course," I answered. "Why?"

"I need a ride. It's an emergency. My mom has a heart condition and I think I just upset her too much. She might be having an attack or something and I want to go check on her. It's ten minutes away."

"Sure," I said. "I'm happy to get out of here, anyway."

He looked back at all the girls at the tables by the stage. "But it's your party. Are you sure this is okay? You're the guest of honor."

I rolled my eyes. "Some honor. Being degraded for the sake of tradition."

In two minutes flat, Donnie had gone to the back room, changed into jeans and a T-shirt, and we were out in the parking lot by my car. I had a problem sliding the key in the lock since the drinks were kicking in.

"Whoa," he commented. "Maybe I should drive."

I looked up at him, my head swimming. "Maybe you should. I'm not drunk, but I'm not sober, either."

"You okay?"

I stared back at him, in total awe that he would stop and be concerned about me when his own mother might be having a heart attack. I'd never met anyone with that kind of caring spirit. I felt myself being drawn to him.

16

"I'm fine," I replied, rushing to the passenger side. "Let's get going. I don't want to keep you from checking on your mom."

As we drove, he told me how close he was to his mother. That his dad died when he was a young boy and now he was the only one left to look out for her. She was sickly and didn't have much money besides her Social Security check. His dad didn't leave behind a will.

"I can't fathom that," he said, turning left down a one-way street. "How can you not have a will if you have a wife and family? My dad was a good man and all—I don't want to speak badly of him—but he left Mom with nothing. She barely gets by. And now her landlord wants to evict her because she's gotten behind on her rent, but I'm not going to let that happen. I'll die before my mom gets turned out on the streets. I'd have her stay with me, but I live in a cramped place with a guy who practices electric guitar until all hours of the morning. I don't think she'd like it too much there."

Maybe it was the booze in my bloodstream, but I felt really comfortable with him. Comfortable enough to share a part of my own life.

"It's nice you have such a loving heart," I said. "I wish the guy I was marrying had the same kind of values that you have. When you said you wouldn't let any girl you gave your heart to go to a place like that strip club, it really hit me. I hate that place. I never wanted to go to that stupid party, but Paul made me feel like such a boring, old stuffed shirt if I didn't go. I guess I did it to make him happy."

Donnie looked over at me with surprise. "Happy? Man, I'd be nuts if my lady was in a strip club. The only naked guy I want her to see is me!"

I reflected back to the awesome build he had, the way his muscles rippled underneath me as he carried me over his shoulder to the throne by the stage. Even in a plain T-shirt and faded jeans as he sat behind the steering wheel of my car, he was drop-dead gorgeous. A heated sensation feathered over me.

"So, you only took this job to help your mom?" I asked. "I didn't mean to eavesdrop on your conversation with her, but—"

"Yeah." He nodded. "It's the only way I can think of to make quick money—legally, anyway. I've got to raise a little over a thousand dollars with less than a week to pay off her late rent and keep her in the apartment. I'm going to quit the club after that. It's not where I belong."

Something inside of me was melting just listening to this guy. He was everything I had ever dreamed of in a man, but thought didn't exist.

"And where do you belong?"

"With kids," he answered, grinning. "Believe it or not, I want to work with special-needs kids. I'm going to go back to school and get my degree in child psychology and see if I can get going in that field."

We arrived at a four-storey brick building where he rushed ahead up the stairs as I trailed behind. I heard him whispering a prayer as he climbed the steps, begging to find his mother safe. As soon as he slid a key from his pocket and opened door number thirty-two, his prayer was answered.

"I'm fine, Donnie." She cackled, embarrassed at all the fuss. "You didn't have to run over here like a lunatic with your lady friend. I'm not that frail that I'm going to drop dead just because I disapprove of your job."

He shrugged awkwardly. "I wanted to check on you. I worry about you, Mom."

She thawed her icy attitude and gave him a big hug. "I'm fine, son. Believe me, I am. Now, don't keep this pretty lady waiting any longer. Maybe if I can't talk you out of working at that dirty club, she can. She looks like a girl with a good head on her shoulders."

We left and the mood was far better. Instead of the tension and rush we were under before, Donnie was greatly relieved and driving slower. I found myself smiling at him and how cute he was with his mother. Paul had a mother in a nursing home three miles from his own place, but rarely went to see her. He claimed he was too busy. I had the feeling Donnie would move mountains before he missed time with his mother, no matter what. The longer I spent with him, the more I realized what a mistake marrying Paul would be. He wasn't the kind of sensitive, caring, and honorable man I had always wanted. Donnie was, actually. Ironic, but true. Even if nothing materialized between us, he at least saved me from making a very permanent mistake.

"I think you're special," I said.

He looked at me and smiled. "Whoa! Those were strong drinks back there."

"No. It's not the drinks. You are special and you've shown me something important. My fiancé is a jerk. I don't want to marry him. I want somebody to love me like you said you'd love your girl. Besides, you can always tell a decent guy by the way he feels about his mother, and you love your mother. That makes you wonderful. I didn't think wonderful guys existed in this world."

He was slightly embarrassed, but appreciated the compliment. "Would you like to have some coffee? My place isn't far from here. I promise I'm harmless and won't make a move."

"What about your guitar-playing roommate?"

"It's Friday night," he answered. "He plays at a bar and won't be home until almost dawn."

I didn't know hours could fly by so fast, but Donnie and I had coffee, listened to music, and even walked out on his terrace to look at the stars. I should've felt guilty about leaving the girls at the club without a word. I should've felt wrong for being with another man besides Paul, but instead I was having a beautiful night. The most beautiful night of my life.

"Can I kiss you?" Donnie asked, the twinkling sky reflected in his eyes.

I didn't even say yes, I just showed him. We kissed forever, finding ourselves starting on the terrace and ending up in his bedroom. I'd never wanted a man more than I wanted Donnie right then. Making love seemed so right. Nothing could've kept us apart. I ended up falling asleep satisfied in his arms and not waking up until morning.

"Where were you?" Paul shouted as I opened my front door that next day. He used his key and even took the liberty of fixing himself a sandwich. I could see the uneaten half sitting on a plate on my coffee table.

I brushed by him. "You wanted me to live a little and I did." I was feeling wonderfully un-guilty.

"Your sisters told me you left last night and never came back. Where did you go?"

It was more than I could take. After spending a night with someone who had a heart and now facing a man who only had his stubborn pride, I had to do what was right.

"Let's just say that I found reality last night," I answered, tipping my chin with confidence. "I could finally see what a mistake this is with you. I don't want this anymore, Paul. The wedding is off. Any man who can happily send me off to be with a room full of naked men for a drunken evening of trouble isn't the kind of man I want to vow my life to."

"What kind of trash is this?" he snapped. "I didn't do anything out of the ordinary. A bachelorette party is nothing, for crying out loud. Everybody has them nowadays."

I met his gaze. "That's not true. There are some men who know the real meaning of a relationship and wouldn't allow the woman they love to stoop so low. I want you to leave, Paul. We're not as compatible as I thought. And you can take your sandwich with you."

There was no pain once he left. No shock or remorse. All I felt was lighter and better than I had in a long time. As much as I cared about Paul, I can honestly say I was never really in love with him. I didn't realize until meeting someone like Donnie that love meant a whole lot more.

The next afternoon, Donnie came over. I'd written my address on a piece of paper for him the night before, praying he'd come by. Once

I saw the look on his face, I knew I wasn't the only one feeling sparks. He couldn't keep himself from smiling.

"Look," he said, stepping into my foyer. "I don't usually take girls to my place and make love when I hardly know them. What happened between us was as sudden and strong as a freight train. I don't know if you were serious when you said you didn't want to marry that guy anymore, but if you were, I'd like to take you out again tonight. Maybe a nice dinner someplace—nothing too fancy. Just somewhere we can talk and maybe sneak a few more kisses in."

"You don't have to be at the club tonight?" I asked, thrilled over his invitation.

"Nope," he answered. "I quit. You won't believe this, but my mom got the money for her back rent and she isn't going to be evicted. We don't even know who gave it to her. The exact amount she needed was in an envelope and shoved under her door this morning. She called me in tears, saying it was a heaven-sent miracle. I have to believe her. I sure can't explain it any other way."

"That's wonderful," I said, reaching out to kiss his cheek. "And I did mean it about Paul. He's gone. It's over. And—yes, I'd love to see you again tonight."

He turned back to the door and then lingered. "Okay, then. How about seven o'clock? Is that okay?"

"Perfect."

Once he left, my legs turned all rubbery. I leaned against the wall and smiled. Maybe later I'd tell him exactly where that money came from. That the nest egg I'd set aside for my honeymoon was far better spent on something with meaning. I certainly felt good about myself having done it. Or, better yet, maybe I'd just let him keep on believing in miracles. I sure was beginning to!

THE END

MY NIGHTMARE NUPTUALS
I was all dressed up with no one to marry

"**W**here is he? Where could he be?" I hissed at my brother. "The wedding was supposed to start ten minutes ago!"

Royce patted my shoulder awkwardly. "Take it easy, Sis. I'm sure he's on his way. Maybe he's having car trouble."

I threw his hand off and began to pace back and forth, the train of my long, white gown billowing out behind me. "If Paul's having car trouble, why hasn't he called? Roy, hand me the phone, please."

I called Paul's cell phone for the tenth time in an hour. Again, all I got was his voicemail.

"Stop pacing—you'll dirty your train. He'll be here, Robin," my mother soothed. But her eyes betrayed her anxiety.

Surely I wasn't being stood up, was I?

A hundred people were seated in the garden of the spectacular mansion we'd rented for the wedding. The sun was shining brightly, making the yellow flowers glow. The carefully chosen symphony music played softly in the background. The minister shifted his weight from one foot to the other as he stood at the head of the altar. People were murmuring and looking at their watches. Soon, the flower girl started chasing the ringbearer. I stared at my three best friends in their lemon-yellow bridesmaid dresses and they smiled back at me nervously. We'd only rented the place for two hours. If Paul didn't arrive soon, we'd have to pack up and leave.

Where, oh, where is Paul? I wondered.

Paul's best friend, Tony, came into the room just then and he looked nervous. I'd always liked Tony. I considered him my buddy, too. We always played darts together at the pub while Paul talked business with people, as he invariably did.

"Um, Robin, can I talk to you for a minute?"

My heart sank. I could tell from his expression that he didn't have good news and I knew what he was going to say. Taking a deep breath, I asked, anyway, "Is Paul coming?"

"I'm sorry."

When devastating things happen you can do one of two things: You can either crawl back in bed and hide or you can do your best to carry on. I decided to carry on.

My parents had already paid for the reception, so I decided to go. A great many of my friends and family had flown in from out of town expecting a party and I wasn't about to let them down.

The reception was a blur. I yanked off the beautiful lace veil that my mother had worn as a bride and pulled the pins out of my hair, letting the curls spill down my back. My friends made sure to keep my champagne glass filled. Guests complimented me on my bravery and my friends loudly condemned Paul for his cowardice. Most of Paul's friends and family left as soon as they found out he wasn't coming.

A part of me longed to be crying in my bedroom, but I held my head up high. All I could think of was, why? Why did Paul not show up for the wedding he was so eager to have?

We'd only been dating for four months when he proposed. He told me that he knew I was the woman he was going to marry the moment he first laid eyes on me. At the time I thought it was incredibly romantic, but was it just a line? Why would he skip out on me after all of this trouble and expense?

Paul's parents were very upset. His mother, Stacey Ann, came and sat beside me and held my hand. "I don't know what got into that son of mine," she cried, "but don't you worry, Robin—I'll make sure he marries you!"

Stacey Ann had always liked me and I knew that she was eager for grandchildren. Was she the reason Paul had proposed so quickly? Had he only wanted to marry me because his mother approved? My head began to ache. It was all too much to think about.

"Please just have Paul call me," I said, pulling my hand away. "I just want to know what happened."

I walked around the room. People seemed to be having a good time. A party is a party, after all. I downed glass after glass of champagne and stuffed myself with mini crab cakes and shrimp cocktails. It all tasted wonderful. I'd been dieting to be able to squeeze myself into my wedding gown, but at that point I figured, what the heck?

We even dug into the wedding cake—a three-tiered, triple-chocolate masterpiece with butter cream frosting that I'd made myself. It was delicious. I picked off the tiny bride and groom figures on top and handed them to the children to play with. There was no sense in keeping them.

I avoided looking at the table piled high with wedding gifts that would have to be returned. I didn't want to think of all those unpleasant details right then. I just wanted to eat, drink, and be merry. There would be plenty of time to cry later on.

The band began to play and people started dancing.

"How are you doing, Robin?" Tony sat down next to me, his green eyes full of sympathy.

"I'm okay." I gave him the same brave smile I'd been flashing all evening. "Can I ask you something? Did he say why? Did Paul explain anything to you at all?" I had an uncomfortable feeling that he might be out with some of his more obnoxious college buddies. A few of them hadn't shown up for the wedding. Maybe they were at a strip club laughing about Paul's narrow escape.

He shrugged uncomfortably. "I don't know what his problem is. He's obviously crazy. Any man would have to be to leave a gorgeous woman like you. Would you like to dance?"

"Why not?"

We stood up and began swaying to the music. Tony isn't as tall as Paul, but he has a more athletic build and his shoulders are broader. I rested my head against his strong chest and he smelled so good. Tony works as a horse trainer and always smells like a combination of horses, leather, and the outdoors.

"You're a really good dancer," I said.

"My mom made me take lessons when I was a kid. Come on, I'll show you some fancy tricks." He spun me around and dipped me. My shoulder-length hair almost touched the floor!

The music sped up and suddenly we were dancing faster. Tony expertly guided me back and forth and I only stepped on his toes a few times. For a brief moment, I forgot that I'd been stood up and actually started having fun. Dancing, to me, has always been a very sexy activity. When all the champagne I'd consumed started to catch up with me, I began to feel a little dizzy and more than a little turned on.

"That was great, but I'm getting winded. I need to sit down," I said to Tony.

"Of course." He helped me over to a comfortable chair and went to fetch a glass of water for me.

It was getting late. All around us people were leaving.

"Darling, Dad and I are going home. Do you want us to drop you off?" my mother asked, looking at me with concern. I'd had an awful lot to drink, but I didn't want to go home just yet. There was nothing to do there but cry into my pillow.

"I'll make sure she gets home okay, Mrs. Stevens," Tony said. My parents were satisfied with that and headed home.

"Oh, good, let's dance some more!" I exclaimed. And we did. Fast songs, slow songs—Tony held his own through them all. I wished we could dance all night long. Finally, it got so late that the band started packing up and the staff began turning off the lights.

"Umm . . . Robin," Tony began.

"Hmm?" My eyes were closed and I was snuggled up in his big, strong arms. I didn't ever want to leave that spot.

"Everyone is just about gone. We should probably get going, too."

"Right. Just a minute." I was drunk and feeling brazen. "I just need to do one more thing."

"What's that?"

That's when I kissed him. He was surprised and broke away. He looked at me for a minute. I'd surprised myself, too, but it felt so right.

"Please?" I asked.

He wrapped his arms around me and kissed me long and deep. He had a wonderful mouth and knew how to kiss just the way I liked. I ran my hands across his muscular back.

"Oh, God," he said. "You're so beautiful, Robin. I want you so much, but this isn't right."

"What?" I asked hazily. I wanted his lips back.

"You're drunk and you're hurting right now. I can't take advantage of you like this." He smoothed my hair back and kissed my forehead. "Believe me, it's not because I don't want to be with you."

"Oh," my face got hot and suddenly I felt very conscious of what I was doing. A rejected bride, I was drunk, disheveled, and hitting on my fiancé's best friend just to make myself feel better. I burned with shame. "I'm sorry," I said. And then, just to make my humiliation complete, I leaned over and threw up on Tony's shoes.

"Ma'am, what would you like to drink?" the stewardess asked me on the plane the next day.

Did I mention that I decided to go on the honeymoon? Why not, right? It was paid for and I wasn't going to let Paul's cold feet cheat me out of going to Hawaii.

"Just bottled water please," I said. I had a vicious hangover. I don't normally drink much—maybe an occasional glass of wine with dinner or a beer or two. My head throbbed as I dug into my bag for some aspirin.

All around me happy couples chatted excitedly. They were looking forward to their vacations. I was happy to be going away, too.

I squirmed all over just thinking about the day before. I'd been left at the altar and all my friends and family were there to see my humiliation.

My deaf grandmother hadn't understood what happened. "What?" she shouted. "Why didn't he show up?"

That was the question. Nobody had been able to get in touch with Paul. After he'd called Tony to tell him that he wasn't coming, he disappeared. My initial feelings of devastation were turning to feelings of anger. How could he do that to me? At the very least he should've talked to me and told me what was going on. Dumping the news on his best friend and then taking off was a rotten thing to do.

And Tony, oh, God! My face burned with shame whenever I thought of him. First I threw myself at him and then I got sick all over him. Luckily, he was a nice guy about it. I put on my headphones, leaned back as far as my seat would allow, and slept all the way to Hawaii.

I've always loved the film Four Weddings And A Funeral, but at that moment I cringed when I thought about the ending. You know—the part where Hugh Grant leaves in the middle of his wedding to go off with Andie McDowell. Not much is made of the way the bride must've felt when she was left standing there all alone. I identified with her and wondered if she went on her honeymoon all alone, too.

The week went by in a flash. I spent my days tanning on the beach, scuba diving, and hiking up the side of a volcano. I had fun during the days, but the nights were hard. I ordered room service in and watched TV alone in the beautiful honeymoon suite. I couldn't help but think about what had happened.

Paul MacArthur was the most beautiful man I'd ever laid eyes on. Ordinarily I don't go for the super-handsome type, but I thought Paul was special. One look at his silky, black hair, sparkling blue eyes, and dimples and I felt like I'd been knocked over the head. I was catering a party at his mother's house when he walked in the door and we looked into each other's eyes for the first time.

"Hi," he said. "Are you the one responsible for all of this glorious food?"

I blushed at the compliment.

Paul swept me off my feet. He's from a wealthy family and is used to having the best of everything. He has an impressive trust fund and dabbles in various businesses. We went to the most expensive restaurants in town, took a glorious vacation to a private island, and went to parties nearly every night. Paul is a mover and a shaker. He knows every person in town and always seems to want to talk business with each and every one of them. In fact, his main occupation seems to be going to parties. If at times I was a little bored at those parties, I was still awed by them because they were usually held at some fabulous estate. After all, as the daughter of a mailman I was thrilled to think that Paul, someone with looks, class, and money, would want to be with someone like me.

While I was packing my bags on the last day of my vacation, the phone rang.

"Hi, sweetie," a familiar voice said.

I nearly dropped the phone. "Paul?"

"I'm so, so, sorry, babe. I screwed up."

"You sure did!" I said, furious. "What's your excuse?"

"I'm sorry, baby. It was just cold feet—the worst kind of cold feet. But I'm ready to fly out right now. We can get married there." He was slurring his words a little.

"Are you drunk? You must be kidding me! There's no way I'd marry you now!" I was seething.

The nerve of him! I thought. How could he wait all this time to call me? His mother must've threatened to cut off his trust fund.

"Robin, please don't be like this." I could hear him trying to muster up some charm. "I love—"

I hung up on him and took the phone off the hook.

As good as it felt to hang up on Paul, there was still a small part of me that wanted him to come out to Hawaii and marry me. Though I longed for a happy ending, I realized that Paul and I aren't really suited. Paul is really nothing but a spoiled child who's used to getting by on his looks and his money. He only wanted a wife to please his parents and possibly to enhance his social standing. And me, well, I think my desire to marry him had really been just the desire to get married. I badly wanted to have a husband and children. Let's face it—at twenty-nine, I wasn't getting any younger.

I found myself wondering about Tony. Tony and Paul had been friends since childhood, but unlike Paul, Tony isn't from a wealthy family. Tony's father was the MacArthur family's chauffeur. I'd always been drawn to Tony's warm and easygoing manner. We have a lot in common. Both of us are couch potatoes who prefer watching movies to going to parties. I thought of him then with a pang of sadness because I doubted that I'd ever see him again since Paul was out of my life for good.

I returned home tanned, rested, and ready to go back to work. One of the best things about being with Paul was that I made a lot of contacts for my catering business. I returned home to a full schedule and it kept me busy. Since I was no longer on a diet, I threw myself into testing—and frequently tasting—a new cake recipe that I call Heartbreak Cake. It's filled with chocolate and caramel—my two favorite comfort foods.

One day not long after I'd returned I was tossing together a new version of the cake when there was a knock on the door.

"Come on in!" I called out. I figured it was my best friend, Jane, who'd been coming over a lot to help me taste the cake.

I wasn't looking my best that day. My hair was falling out of a loose ponytail and I was wearing gray sweatpants and an old T-shirt. My face was covered with flour and I wasn't wearing a stitch of makeup. When Paul and I were together he wanted me to look glamorous twenty-four hours a day, so it was nice to go back to my sloppy ways.

When I came out of the kitchen I nearly dropped my mixing bowl. There stood Tony, his blond hair glowing golden in the sunlight that was streaming in my windows. He looked like a young Robert Redford standing there in his jeans and cowboy boots. He looked even more delicious than my Heartbreak Cake.

"Hi." He stood there awkwardly with his hands in his pockets.

"Sorry to interrupt. I just wanted to check on you and see how you're doing."

"Oh, thanks. I mean, I'm glad you're here," I stammered. "Please, come into the kitchen. I'm just having some cake. Would you like some?"

It was hard to look at him. He was so gorgeous and I remembered how the last time he saw me, I was barfing on his shoes.

I babbled on about the beauty of Hawaii while I cut and served the cake. "Would you like some coffee with that?" I asked.

"Sure," he said. "I'm glad you had a good time. You look a lot happier than the last time I saw you."

We both blushed at that.

"I'm sorry that Paul treated you so badly," he continued. "You deserve so much more. But I have to confess, I'm glad that you didn't get married. I never thought you guys were well suited for each other."

"Oh, no? Do you know a guy more suitable for me?" I teased.

"As a matter of fact, I do. He's not wealthy and he can't shower you with diamonds, but he's always had the biggest crush on you." Tony's green eyes glowed. "And he'd really like to kiss you right now." His lips brushed mine gently and then he gave me a passionate kiss.

I got my happy ending. It wasn't the one I'd planned on, but in the end it suited me better. Being dumped on my wedding day actually turned out to be one of the best things that ever happened to me.

THE END

MARRIAGE MANIA
I had everything but the groom

I shopped for furniture, china, carpets, and towels. I was constantly planning my future dream home and what the living room, bedrooms, kitchen, and baths would be like.

I knew the flowers I'd have in the flower beds, down to the beds of pansies that would line the front walk. I could see the smoke trailing out of the chimney on a frosty evening, the table set with our good everyday china, the meal hot and steamy from my stove. My husband, dreamy and sexy, walking up the steps, anxious to get home to me.

But the dream was just a dream. I could work and save and pick up an item or two here and there, but fine china and fireplaces were a long way from where I was. That dreamy, sexy husband was nowhere on the horizon.

My best friend, Gloria, and I had an apartment together. We worked at office jobs, had been friends throughout high school, and couldn't wait until we were on our own. We'd bought frugally for our two bedroom apartment, saving what little we could for our future dream homes. We both had those. But Gloria had something I didn't have. She had Tony, her fiancé, and an engagement ring he'd given her the night of our graduation. She and Tony knew what they wanted and were in such solid agreement that sometimes it was hard to tell where one ended and the other began.

I have to admit I was envious. Gloria was closer to me than my sister. And Tony acted as if he were my big, goofy brother. I was happy for her, really I was. But I couldn't help feeling left behind. Where was my Romeo? How was I ever to find him?

No one had come along to share my dreams. I'd gone out with a few guys, but either I thought they were creeps after a date or two, or I found them attractive and they didn't call me back. I just couldn't connect with anyone.

I hated going to family reunions where everyone seemed as paired up as Noah's ark. An aunt or two always managed to ask where "my beau" was.

Mother used to take my side. "She's too young," she'd say. "She's wise to wait." But lately even she had quit making excuses.

Then Rob came along. We met through work, kind of. Rob worked for the company in the office building next to ours. I couldn't believe it when my coworker, Denise, said she had a blind date for me. I'd never even considered going out on a blind date. I always figured

I'd get matched up with someone really weird. But Denise asked me and promised that Rob, my date-to-be, was a really nice guy. He'd seen me leave work with her and wanted to know who I was and if I had a husband. When he found out I didn't have one, he wanted a date. So Denise arranged for us to meet at a Chinese restaurant.

Denise said Rob was nervous about meeting me. Him nervous? At that point I didn't know anything about him. I had no idea what to expect. She kept saying he was "nice," but "nice" covers a lot of territory.

I got to the restaurant after changing clothes a few dozen times. I didn't want to wear work-type clothes. I didn't want to wear anything too dressy or too casual. Nothing I had seemed right. I eventually settled on a semi-dressy pant suit.

I kept thinking: Don't get too excited. This will be another episode of either me liking him and him not calling me back, or his being a real creep.   But with all the positive self-talk, I still arrived at the restaurant scared to death.

When the hostess led me to his table, I thought she'd made a mistake. A tall man stood up, dressed in a light blue shirt. He had eyes that sparkled. He was very handsome and looked like a movie star. I couldn't believe it. I blushed, thinking that the hostess had made a mistake and hoping my real date wasn't watching. We'd both end up embarrassed.

I started to say we had the wrong table when he held out his hand to take mine and softly said, "Sally." His eyes locked on mine.

My stomach fluttered. I immediately wished I'd worn a sexier outfit, but he didn't seem to notice what I had on. His eyes never left my face.

"Please sit," he said as the hostess pulled out my chair.

We sat down, leaving the menus lying on the table, both of us looking at each other.

"I'm so glad you decided to come," he said, his eyes twinkling in the candlelight. He was just so breathtaking. "I was afraid you wouldn't."

I swallowed and tried to find my voice. His eyes were so mesmerizing that I couldn't think. He took charge and led us into a conversation, easing my nervousness a bit.

We managed to make small talk until the waiter came to take our order. Then we realized we hadn't even looked at the menus.

We laughed and quickly ordered, the waiter first looking at Rob then at me, I guess thinking we'd lost our minds.

Somehow we ate, paid, and left. It seemed a blur, a dream. I'll always remember that night—how the candle flickered on the table, the light dancing across us. His eyes were so remarkable and his smile was so endearing. He seemed intent on pleasing me, making sure everything was just right.

All I wanted to do was study him—take in his face, his hands, how he moved, the way he laughed. Then I wanted to get to know him. I wanted to know everything about him, but I didn't want to appear nosy or too eager. So I was quiet before I asked him any questions. He seemed to take this as a sign of intelligence. He said, "I don't think I've ever dated anyone as smart as you."

I blushed and quickly denied what he was saying.

"No, I mean it. You think about what you're saying. Most women just chatter on and on, going from one thing to another. It makes my head spin. But you pace yourself. I like that."

By the end of the evening, when Rob had left me at the front door of my apartment, I thought I might've found my soul mate. He kissed me gently on the lips, brushed his fingers against my hair, and whispered, "This has been a very special evening for me. I hope you'll consider going out with me again."

I nodded, unable to breathe. He was more than I ever expected. And he was so sincere.

Gloria was home, and I told her all about him.

"I've never seen you so excited about anyone," she said, happy that I had a good time.

"This could be it." Then I shook my head. "No, I take that back. I don't want to say anything to jinx this. I want to be level-headed and sure." Then I sighed. "But he is so sexy."

Gloria laughed.

Rob and I began to see each other on a regular basis. We had a standing dinner date every Friday night, sometimes even meeting for lunch through the week. We never ran out of things to talk about.

He traveled to his mother's on Saturdays to spend the weekend with her, saying that she was ill and couldn't get around very easily and she needed him. I'd always heard that a son who visits his mother is a keeper. He sometimes apologized that we couldn't do things on the weekend, but I enjoyed the times we did get together.

Before long, my dream to have a home with just the right furniture, the right garden, and now the right husband was growing. When Gloria was free, we'd shop. On Sunday afternoons we'd sometimes go to open houses, looking at homes to get ideas and see what was on the market, what houses had what, what certain neighborhoods looked like. I even thought we could find a home with a mother-in-law apartment. His mother could be near us. I wanted to meet her. I wanted her to like me.

Gloria and Tony were moving along with their plans. They'd agreed to work a year, save their money, then get married.

That would mean I'd have the apartment all to myself, but with the way Rob and I were progressing, I hoped we could make similar plans.

Gloria kept pleading for me to have Rob over so that she and Tony could get to know him, so the next week I invited him for dinner at the apartment. I hoped that the four of us would get along.

Thursday night I cleaned and arranged things, patting the throw pillows a dozen times. After work on Friday I stopped to pick up groceries. Tony had agreed to grill steaks. Gloria and I made a salad, and I threw together an apple pie that my mother had taught me to make.

Everything was ready and I was so nervous that my stomach was fluttering and my palms were sweaty. I wasn't too worried that Gloria wouldn't like Rob. But I wanted Tony and Rob to get along.

Rob showed up looking great as usual. He and Tony hit it off immediately, both quickly finding out they were sports nuts. Gloria signaled me to join her in the kitchen.

As soon as we were out of sight, Gloria said, "I didn't realize he's so cute."

I nodded. "I know, I know. I'm so glad he and Tony are getting along."

She grabbed my hand and gave it a squeeze. "This is so great. The four of us forever."

Rob and Tony took over the grill, talking sports, steaks, and I don't know what else.

When we finally sat down to eat, Gloria and I were starting to feel left out. Rob complimented us on the beautiful meal, gave me a wink, and we ate.

Rob asked Gloria a few questions about her work, her family, and by the time we were clearing off the table, he was teasing her the way Tony teased me sometimes.

The evening couldn't have gone better. I awoke the next morning on cloud nine.

"You want to go shopping?" I asked Gloria at breakfast.

"What did you have in mind?" she asked.

"Oh, I don't know. Maybe bedroom furniture."

Gloria laughed.

We spent the day shopping, planning, talking, picturing rosy futures with big houses, green lawns, and happy children playing on swing sets.

Over the next few weeks, we double-dated with Tony and Gloria. We all had similar interests, and I was beginning to think it was time for Rob to meet my parents. I'd told Mom about him, that he was nice and we were seeing each other. I'd made it sound casual. I didn't want the family to start making wedding plans. I could see Aunt Elaine putting our picture and an announcement in the paper without our permission.

So I'd decided that I would bring it up with Rob for the next Friday night.

Only Rob had different plans. I asked him what we were going to do. I was hoping we were going out to dinner, because lately we'd been eating at the apartment a lot, and Gloria and Tony were starting to feel a little put out. They wanted the place to themselves from time to time, but Rob liked coming there.

No one had said anything outright, but the last couple of Fridays Gloria had been less than warm when I said Rob and I were eating at home. I saw her push Tony out the door quickly, but I really didn't spend a lot of time thinking about it.

When I mentioned Friday night to Rob, he said, "Oh, I'm going to the basketball game Friday night."

"You are? Were you going to say anything to me about it?"

He was quiet for a minute, then he smiled and said, "Sure, I just forgot. This came up, and I said I'd go. I knew you'd understand."

I didn't, but I smiled and said that I did.

So on Friday night I was stuck at home, by myself, for the first time in a long time and it seemed really strange. Gloria and Tony had gone to the game, too.

I thought it would be a good time to get some things done, but I found myself feeling a bit uneasy. I'd become so used to having Rob around on Fridays that it was hard being by myself again.

Frankly I didn't like it, and I hoped that next time Rob would ask me to go along. While basketball wasn't something I particularly enjoyed, I could go and be interested, just the way I expected Rob to do things I might like to do, like see a play or a concert.

When Gloria got up the next morning, she was very quiet. I asked her if she was feeling bad, and she said, "Just a little."

She kept glancing at me out of the corner of her eye.

"What is it?" I finally asked.

"Tony and I saw Rob at the ball game," she said.

"You did? I think someone from his work asked him to go."

"Really? He wasn't with anyone when we saw him. In fact, he sat with us." Her voice had a funny tone.

"Maybe whoever it was couldn't go at the last minute." I knew there had to be an explanation. I couldn't understand why Gloria was acting as though it was such a big deal.

"Maybe," was all she answered.

Over the next few days I expected Rob to call, but he didn't. On top of that, Gloria wasn't acting her usual self. I hoped she and Tony weren't having problems. I was afraid that the closer it got to their wedding date, the more nervous they might get.

So I said something to her one day. "Are you and Tony okay?"

She said, "Yeah, just fine. How's Rob?"

"I was just getting ready to call him to find out. He hasn't called all week."

Gloria never said a word. Then the phone rang. It was Rob.

"How are you doing?" he asked.

"Fine. I was just getting ready to call you. I was beginning to think you might be sick or something."

"Why would you think that?" he asked, and I caught an edge in his voice.

"I haven't heard from you in a few days. How's your mother?"

"I've been busy," he said, not answering my question.

"Was the ball game good?"

"Yes, it was. I had more fun than I thought I would."

"Who did you say asked you to go?"

There was silence for a moment or two. During that time I felt like a nosy, nagging girlfriend and I instantly wished I hadn't said a thing. But a gnawing feeling made me wonder why he was being so cagey.

He said, "I have to go. I'll see you later." He hung up before I could even say a word.

After work I had to run by the store and pick up some groceries. It was my turn to buy. I pulled into the drive. Rob's car was there. When he said he'd see me later, I didn't realize he meant that afternoon.

I checked my hair in the mirror, grabbed my groceries, and headed inside.

When I opened the door, I was surprised by the scene. Gloria was standing near the kitchen doorway. She looked furious. Her eyes were wide and her lips were tight. Rob, on the other hand, looked mischievous, like a carefree teenager lounging on the sofa, grinning.

"Hey guys," I said, a little hesitant. I held out my grocery bag to Rob. "You want to give me a hand? I could whip up something pretty quick."

Rob looked at the bag and made no move to take it. "No, I have to run. Can't stay. See you." He stood and hurried out the door, brushing past me.

"Rob," I called out after him, but he kept right on going as if I hadn't said a word.

I turned back to Gloria, who had tears running down her face.

"What is it? What's the matter? You want to tell me what's going on?" I asked, completely flustered by the scene I'd walked in on.

Gloria shook her head. She took a deep breath and looked down. "I don't want to tell you this at all. But I have to." Her voice was shaky.

I waited for her to begin.

"Oh, I hate this." She shook her head again, as if clearing her mind. "But you need to know." She tried to look at me, but her eyes were all over the room. "I think Rob is the biggest creep I've ever met in my life."

My mouth dropped open. I couldn't believe my ears. "How can you say that? You know how I feel about him."

She gulped and choked back more tears. "I know, I know. That's what makes this so horrible. He's just not the guy you think he is." She leaned against the wall.

"First of all, all those weekends he was going to see his mother? Other women. You're by no means the only girlfriend he has. He even joked that you were his Girl Friday. He has a Girl Saturday. Get the picture?"

"That's ridiculous. What makes you think that?" I demanded.

"People have told me, and I believe them."

"You! You always want evidence before you believe gossip. Why would you want to believe something awful about Rob? You've been with him. You see how he is. Does he seem like someone like that?"

"Believe me, I don't want to say bad things about Rob, not to you. I wondered why he went to the ball game that night without you. I wondered why we didn't all go together. Tony told me to keep quiet. He knew something then."

"I don't understand."

"No one asked him to go. He wanted to go by himself. He flirted with every girl there. And he made a big deal about it in front of us. He wanted me and Tony to see him talking to other girls. I was so miserable. We left before the game was over just to get away from him."

I didn't want to believe her. She was mistaken. Gloria had always been kind of prudish. Rob was probably being outgoing and friendly, and she saw it as flirting. She thought when two people were a couple they should put on blinders and never look at anyone of the opposite sex.

"Gloria, I believe in Rob. We're going to get married. He's the one. I know it. The four of us will grow old together. Just wait and see."

"Has he asked you to marry him?" she asked.

"No, not in so many words, but I know he's getting ready to. We haven't been seeing each other that long. Those things take time. I'm going to take him to meet Mom and Dad."

"Don't," she said.

I couldn't believe her. What in the world was happening to my best friend? I was beginning to get mad at her. "Gloria, please don't say another word. You're going to make me angry if you keep going on about this. I know Rob."

34

"He asked me out," she blurted out. "Twice. In fact, that's what he was doing when you showed up. I'd just told him off."

I stared at Gloria. The words she was saying were not reaching my brain. I knew she was saying something really awful, but I couldn't understand it.

She reached out to me, but I pushed her away.

"Get out!" I screamed. "Get out!" I was so mad that I threw the groceries on the floor.

Gloria's eyes grew large and she tried to calm me down. "Please," she started.

"Get away from me!" I yelled. "You did this."

Gloria's face went white. Then she shook her head and went to her bedroom.

I picked up the groceries and took them to the kitchen, part of me thinking that if I did something ordinary, this unreal experience would go away.

I put away the groceries and tried to calm my nerves. None of this was making any sense. Gloria and I had been friends for as long as I could remember. We agreed on the same things, liked the same things. As I walked back to the living room, I thought that might be the problem. Gloria and I could no longer be roommates. I should've seen that she was jealous of me and Rob. She'd dated only Tony since her high school days. She'd never dated a real man. I'm sure Rob, with his sexiness and charm, just got the best of her. She wanted what I had.

The best thing for her to do would be to go ahead and move in with Tony. I would stay, and then Rob and I could have the apartment. We could be there whenever we wanted without feeling that we were putting anyone out. Now I could see that those looks Gloria was giving when Rob and I showed up were pure jealousy.

We'd been friends for so long that I couldn't believe she would undermine me like this. But infatuation can make people do strange things. Gloria had let her emotions make her a little crazy. No wonder Tony was uneasy about Rob being over so much. He probably sensed that Gloria was beginning to have feelings for Rob. That would explain why Tony didn't want Gloria around Rob at the ball game, why they left early. Tony wouldn't ordinarily leave a ball game before it was over.

I straightened the living room and grabbed my purse. I decided to go see Rob and find out exactly what had happened between him and Gloria. I'd let him know that she wouldn't be in our way any longer.

I left a note for Gloria that said I wanted her out of the apartment when I got back. She could pick up her things later.

As I drove over to Rob's, I thought about Gloria and her saying that Rob was flirting with all the women at the game. She must've been trying to cause problems between me and Rob then. She was trying to make me jealous. And I had thought she wanted the best for me. Now I understood why she had been acting so differently lately. She hadn't been herself for several weeks. Her tone had changed. She was constantly watching me out of the corner of her eye.

I pulled into Rob's drive, but he wasn't there. I left a note for him to call, drove by his office to see if he had gone back to work for some overtime, then drove by the gym where I knew he liked to work out. I couldn't find him anywhere.

I went back to the apartment. Gloria had gone. I called Rob again. And again. I tried until midnight. But he never answered his phone.

The next morning I tried to catch up with him at his office. I waited in his hallway until it was almost time for me to get to work. I was going to be late. At the last minute, I headed out the door, wondering if Rob's mother might me ill. He hurried in, his shirt looking crisp, his hair damp from a shower. I smiled at him, but he didn't smile back.

I tried to talk to him. "Rob, I need to tell you something."

He stopped for a minute, looked at me, and said, "I don't have a minute right now. I'm going to be late."

"Call me." I tried to grab his hand to give it a squeeze, but he just nodded and went on.

All day I waited for him to call. At lunch I went to his building and waited for him to come out. I thought we could eat together, but I missed him.

All afternoon, all I could think of was telling him that Gloria was now out of the picture and wouldn't be causing trouble anymore.

After work, I tried to catch him again, but I didn't run into him.

I drove by his apartment on the way home, but his car wasn't there. I drove by the gym again. No such luck. I headed home, hoping it'd be there, but he wasn't.

The apartment looked deserted when I entered it. I looked around and noticed several things missing. I walked back to Gloria's room. It was totally empty. She had taken the day to move out.

I called Rob again and again. Finally, at ten o'clock, he picked up the phone. I said, "Hey, sugar, I've been trying to reach you. I really want to talk."

"What about?" he asked, a coolness in his voice.

"Is someone there?" I asked. "Am I catching you at a bad time?"

There was a moment or two of silence. Then he said, "No, it's not a bad time."

"Well, I wanted to tell you that Gloria has moved out. We can use the apartment any time we want."

"Moved out? Why did she do that?"

"I told her to. I think it's best if she's not around when you come by. I think she's got a crush on you."

"She has a funny way of showing it."

"What do you mean?"

"When I asked her to go out with me, she turned me down."

I couldn't breathe. Did he say that? "You asked her out?" I whispered.

"Yep. I thought we could have a good time together. But I guess she's pretty stuck on Tony."

"Why did you do that, Rob? I thought we meant something to each other." Blood was rushing in my ears. I could barely breathe.

"You were fun for a while, but all bad habits have to be stopped at some time."

"I was a bad habit?" My stomach felt awful. I thought I might faint.

"Don't take it the wrong way, hon. We had a couple of dates, some laughs. Now it's time to move on."

I felt sick to my stomach. He couldn't be saying this.

"I thought we had something serious," I said, hating the tone in my voice, wishing I could sound as cool as he was sounding. But my world was crumbling apart and I was scrambling for a way to keep it together, to keep him from saying these things. Something was wrong, but it could be fixed.

"We had some fun, hon. That's all. Look, I have to go."

"No, Rob, don't do this. I know we can make it. Tell me what to do."

"There's nothing you can do. This is just the way it is. It's time for me to move on to someone else."

"Is there someone else? Have you been seeing another woman?" I asked, jealousy already eating me alive.

He laughed. "See you, babe." He hung up.

I was sick, physically and emotionally. The phone felt useless in my hand. I dropped it.

I loved him. He was everything I ever wanted. My dreams had finally all come together, almost. Now they seemed light years away again.

It couldn't be over, just like that. There had to be a way to reach him.

I began a sickening routine of following him, calling him, driving by his apartment, his work, the gym, anywhere I thought I might run into him. If I could just see him, see his smile, everything would be okay.

I finally went to his office one morning, trying to talk to him before he got in. He was standing there in one of his blue shirts, laughing at something someone was saying. He glanced my way, saw me, and excused himself for a minute.

"What are you doing here?" he demanded in a loud whisper.

"I want you to come by this afternoon. We have to talk."

He grabbed my elbow and steered me toward the lobby. "Don't come by here, don't call me. Just leave me alone," he ordered.

He gave me a little shove and turned away.

I looked at his retreating back. Several people were watching. My face turned red. I felt like such a loser.

I drove back home and called in sick. I spent the day crying. I paced and cried. I looked at Gloria's empty room, where the sound of my crying echoed in my ears.

This time I'd lost everything. Rob, my dreams, but most of all, my best friend. I wondered if she'd ever forgive me. I called her that night.

"I'm so sorry, Gloria. I've been a real idiot. You were right about Rob. I just couldn't see it."

She didn't say a word.

"I won't blame you if you never speak to me again," I said. "I just wanted to let you know how sorry I am, and I wish you the best with Tony."

"It's okay. I know you've been hurt."

I felt better. At least she was talking to me again.

"Tony and I have set a date. Still going to be my maid of honor?" she asked.

I burst into tears. "Of course."

I pushed away all my dreams, finally learning to live one day at a time. That's the way life should be lived. Gloria and Tony married and planned for their future. I'm still living in the apartment and working. I've decided to take up some hobbies to fill my time. For now, men and dating are off limits.

THE END

BIG-CITY BRIDE,
COUNTRY-BOY GROOM
Each day, I'm learning to love his world

I never imagined I'd fall in love with a fisherman with Norwegian ancestry—let alone one who lived in Dundas, a Minnesota town the size of a postage stamp. Steve and I met at a party given by mutual friends and though the attraction was instantaneous, the distance between our worlds seemed vast.

Born and raised in Minneapolis, my metropolitan soul was lost in the open farmland and small-town way of life. Bred in the heart of the valley, Steve balked at the noise and congestion of the twin cities. But, love conquers all boundaries and eventually Steve reeled me in with a proposal of marriage and lifelong bliss.

The first month of our engagement passed by in a whirl as we shared our joy with family and friends while adjusting to the new status of our relationship. Then the full impact flowed in with the force of a summer tornado. Skies darkened when we had to decide where the nuptials would occur. It meant a great deal to Steve to be married in his hometown. In my desire to appease my future husband, I agreed to a wedding in Dundas. Only for the life of me, I couldn't figure out why.

What on earth did I know about organizing a small-town wedding? How would I manage from the plush office of my employer in St. Paul? I'd fallen hook and line, but no doubt, now I would definitely be sinking.

Picking the church proved effortless as we naturally gravitated toward the one Steve's family attended. My first real education on Dundas weddings came when I began to investigate catering halls. First and foremost, there weren't any facilities large enough to accommodate our list of expected guests. One evening, I brought up the idea of getting married in the nearby town of Northfield, a larger, college town with ample accommodations. I received a resounding, "No." So my choices became Tavern A or Tavern B, the only businesses with any amount of space, but when I called to inquire about availability, I found that neither of them offered catering options or a setup fit for a reception.

Frazzled and nearly ready to throw in my prenuptial towel, I was saved by a phone call from Steve's mother, who offered to help. Relieved to have the support, I almost missed the kicker of her offer—

"help" meant having the reception on their farm.

Steve's parents owned a picturesque plot of land off the beaten trail, so far off the traveled path that it required a tour guide to find the homestead. Now, it wasn't that I just could see our guests driving aimlessly through the countryside, fruitlessly searching for our event, I really couldn't see them prancing around the dirt in heels and attire sure to rival the outfits we wore to the prom. Traditionally, in my circle, weddings were not treated as a casual affair and I expected everyone would dress to the nines. Would they forgive me for a field wedding? And, heavens, what if it rained that day? The picture of satin and silks scrunched into the cow-milking barn pushed me over the edge into the land of hysteria.

I resigned myself to meet with Steve's mother and let her down easy, after which Steve and I would need to have a serious discussion. The wedding plans brought to light yet another unexplored topic— where would we be living after our marriage? My bliss wasn't just soaked through. It was saturated.

That weekend I drove down to Dundas with a heavy heart. When I snaked through the back roads and arrived at the farm, I was surprised to see Steve's truck along with ten or so other vehicles parked outside his parents' home. As I parked my car, another pulled in alongside mine. Maybe I had the wrong day? I stepped out and a thin, elderly lady from the other vehicle bounded toward me. She grabbed my arm and pulled me towards the house with an unexpected strength.

"You must be Tiffany. We've heard so much about you and I dare say, you're the very picture of what we wished for our Stevie. Come on inside, there's so much to be done. Oh, how exciting! I just love a good wedding!"

I slipped my arm from her grasp and must have looked at her like she'd sprouted green hair, as she made a quick apology and announced that she's Steve's aunt. When I followed her up the steps and into the house, the fresh-baked scent of apple strudel sent my taste buds into a tizzy. The kitchen was full of women fixing plates and chattering about everything from our wedding to the damage inflicted on the soybean crops by the early frost.

"Ahem!" Steve's aunt cleared her throat loudly. "She's here!"

All at once a team of clucking women who half-guided, half-shoved me into a kitchen chair surrounded me. I searched for Steve frantically, but he evidently—and smartly—chose to avoid the chaotic tag teams. My nerve to call off the farm reception grew thin in the face of so many challengers so I simply sat, listened to their well-intentioned suggestions, and politely submitted to their probing questions.

Before I realized the transformation, I found myself chatting freely, nibbling on apple strudel, and paying close attention to the customs and ideas presented. Steve's relatives, neighbors, and family friends surprised me with their creativity and generous offers to set up and cook for our reception. The kitchen filled with goodwill and excitement for our union, so much so that I began to see having the entire wedding, including the ceremony, being held on the farm as a viable option. A tear escaped my eye as I realized how fortunate I was to be marrying into this close-knit, caring community. In all my twenty-four years, I'd never imagined such moments existed outside of Little House on the Prairie reruns. A new world blossomed within my soul.

Steve's mother quietly watched as I discretely wiped the small trail of tears from my cheek before speaking softly to me. "Have we done something wrong, dear? Overwhelmed you too much? I know we can be busybodies at times." She patted my arm and another tear slipped from the corner of my eye.

"It's not that. This is a bit overwhelming, but . . . this is all so wonderful." I stumbled, searching for the right words to convey my gratitude and newfound sense of belonging but failed to find anything adequate to say.

Steve's mother placed her hand over mine and gave it a quick squeeze. "I suppose you should've been warned. You're not just marrying Steve, you know. You're marrying a family. Speaking of which, we've been so busy lollygagging that we forgot the most important thing."

There's more? Will they be offering to make my wedding dress next? I have no doubt that they can pull it off with panache.

"We Dundas women have a tradition we hope you'll uphold."

"Oh. What is that?" Something borrowed, something blue?

"The day before any Dundas wedding, we get together for a fishing trip and it's customary for the bride to join us."

Fishing trip? Wouldn't that involve hooks and slimy creatures of the sea? Even though I'm in love with an avid fisherman, I never tried the sport myself. Leave it to the women in the "Land of 10,000 Lakes" to come up with that wedding tradition!

"Uhm, I guess that would be okay. Though there may be some last-minute details to take care of and I'm not quite certain yet when we'll have the rehearsal dinner."

"Oh, that won't be a bother, dear." Steve's mother looked down the bridge of her nose, communicating clearly that she saw right through my veiled reluctance. "I imagine you don't have too many Bohemian fishing circles in Minneapolis, but I promise you, you'll enjoy the experience. Will you come?"

Every eye in the room trained on me, waiting for my cave-in of acceptance. I nodded and the smiles flashed over their faces in a wave. Why not? What harm could honoring a tradition that obviously meant a great deal to these ladies bring?

On the day before my wedding, I pried myself out of bed at five o'clock in the morning to meet the women of Dundas on Roberds Lake. With bleary eyes and a map in hand, I wound my way through the countryside. An unusual sense of serenity filled me as I reviewed a mental checklist of wedding to-dos. Flowers scheduled for drop off. Check. Tuxedos picked up. Check. Down the list I went as each mile marker disappeared and the sun began its slow climb over the open fields.

The months leading up to the wedding were stressful and hectic, but the support I received from Steve's family and friends softened the impact dramatically. After a number of conversations, Steve and I decided to build a home in Dundas and give it a go, with the condition of renegotiating a move to the cities if the commute or small town living weighed too heavily on me. Still a little leery that I may not adjust, I welcomed the loophole out of country life. All in all, I had no complaints and was far-removed from the frazzled bride I'd expected to be.

As I approached Roberds Lake, the cool scent rolling off the water drifted into the car window, sweeping the last trace of sleep from my eyes. I felt energized and ready to take on the world—or at least the fish, even if I still didn't have a clue how to do it.

Two seconds later, I wasn't quite sure if I was ready to take on the Dundas women, though. The parking lot across the street from the resort docks they'd reserved was so full that the overflow of cars lined the rural highway for at least a hundred feet in either direction. I eased my car in behind the last truck parked and glanced over toward the docks. A crowd full of flannels and windbreakers huddled en masse. Dundas has a population of around 542 residents. By my visual count, somewhere around half of them surrounded Roberds Lake.

I edged up to the tail end of the group and anxiously searched for a familiar face. Will all these people be visiting our wedding reception, too? We haven't planned for nearly enough food. Finally, I caught sight of Steve's mother sitting on the far pier. I walked over and tapped her on the shoulder. She looked up from her fishing pole and a huge grin splashed across her weathered face, lighting it up brighter than the rising, bulbous sun.

"Tiffany! You found us." She stood up and handed her rod to a lady seated nearby. "Look everyone, Tiffany is here!"

A cheer rose up from the women in a simultaneous boom certain to scare away any trace of fish from the area. Someone slipped a flannel blanket over my shoulders and suddenly a swarm of women danced up and down the pier, patting various patches of the blanket as they passed.

"Ouch!" the exclamation escaped my lips as a sharp object pinched my arm. I whirled around to see the source of the pain and something struck my cheek. Tears welled up, involuntarily snaking down my cheek over the sharp cut. Lures. They're hanging fishing lures on me! What type of sadists are these people? What happened to the caring community?

"Ow! Please, wait. Stop."

"That's enough, girls. Hold on," Steve's mother commanded and the crowd stilled. "Oh, dear, that's quite a gash. Nora, run and fetch the first aid kit in my toolbox."

A gash on my cheek the day before my wedding. Fishing lures draped along my body. Was I supposed to be the bait? Were they going to throw me in the lake next? The surreal nature of the torment began spinning me into meltdown.

"Oh, Tiffany, I'm so sorry." Steve's mother looked like the wind had been kicked out of her. "We should've prepared you for this. I'm afraid we got a little carried away."

You could say that again. "It's okay." Not. Maybe marrying a small-town boy was a big mistake. Could I really handle these quirky, tight-knit people? Clearly, I dangled on the outside of the Dundas in-crowd. And right now, that appeared to be a blessing. Who in the heck hung fishing lures on a bride-to-be?

"Perhaps I should explain," Steve's mother offered. The woman she'd referred to as Nora returned with a first aid kit and the both women began fussing over my face.

"Tiffany," my future mother-in-law—maybe my future mother-in-law. At that moment I had my doubts—continued, "We're terribly sorry we startled you. I should've explained everything ahead of time. You see the quilt on your shoulders? We patterned and stitched it over the past few months from scraps of Steve's old fishing jackets and childhood clothing."

I looked down at the blanket. Where I only saw flannel before, the intricate pattern and handcrafted designs leapt out, stunning my vision with their elaborate beauty. An ornate replica of Steve's parents' farm filled a square and an intricate rendition of what appeared to be Steve and I cutting our wedding cake filled another. All around the blanket lay square after square of complex renderings of memories and future blessings. A gush of tears rolled from my eyes but they did not stem from the pain of the wound.

"And the lures?"

"They are for luck and prosperity. It's customary to wish your lives together to be as abundant with love as the countless number of fish who swim in our lakes, and to provide you with a symbol of the tools that will help guide you to catch your fill. Each lure is hand-made and, really, they symbolize that we are here to guide you. We are you tools."

Steve's mother applied an alcohol swab to my cheek but the sting paled in comparison to the overwhelming thankfulness welling in my soul. These women who hardly knew me and inadvertently stuck me with lures were in reality welcoming me into their fold. The same as they had when we'd hit a glitch in our plans for the wedding reception. What an incredible community I'd stumbled into. For the second time I was awash with amazement and filled with gratitude. Crazy fisherwomen or not, they were chock full of hospitality and heart.

The following day I would officially seal my membership in the Dundas circle and whether cover-up would conceal the mark on my face or not, I'd bear it proudly as I walked the aisle to meet Steve.

I threw my arms around his mother and gave her a big squeeze, hoping to convey my gratitude, not just to her but also to all the women on the pier. In that moment I knew they'd made a die-hard fishing fool out me.

Steve and I still live in Dundas and long after our wedding, our beautiful quilt, complete with lures, hangs in a prominent spot on our living room wall as a continued reminder of our family heritage and the town that captured my heart. Each year when there's an engagement announced, I look forward to tormenting a new bride and helping the other women in Dundas ensure that she's a worthy catch.

THE END

SOMETHING BORROWED
Best man steals bride!

"Going down?" Dustin Roche, my fiancé's best man, asked me as I got on the elevator.

"Yes, please," I said as nicely as I could. I knew that Dustin didn't like me, and that he'd be very happy if he could break up my relationship with Daniel, his friend.

But it didn't look like even he could do that. Indeed, I was beginning to feel like Daniel and I were truly blessed. There had even been rumors of a hurricane headed our way, but the day had dawned sunny and calm—a good omen for my wedding tomorrow.

Still, lots of people who lived along this beachfront stretch had boarded up their homes, just in case. Around these parts, there were lots of hurricane warnings. Fortunately, few storms seemed to actually hit land.

I'd grown up here and this was where I wanted to be married. My family had booked a whole floor of rooms in the grand little hotel just across from the beach. The hotel had been around forever; my dad had worked there back when he was in high school. So had Dustin.

Dustin and I had been like oil and water for most of our lives. He was the awful boy who could always find a big bug or a frog to put in my book bag. He'd been the first one to tease me when I was trying out for ballet or basketball. All through my growing-up years, there had been Dustin Roche with a funny comment made mostly at my expense.

So, needless to say, I wasn't exactly thrilled to discover that my fiancé's best friend was none other than Dustin. I think I even groaned out loud when Daniel told me.

"No. Not Dustin Roche. Say it isn't true, Daniel."

"What's wrong with Dustin? I was planning on asking him to be my best man."

I must've groaned again. I tried to tell Daniel about all the tricks Dustin had pulled on me when we were kids.

"But that was a long time ago," Daniel said, laughing. "Krista, it isn't like you to hold a grudge. Besides, you won't be seeing much of him. There's the rehearsal, the ceremony, and then you and I will be flying off to Mexico. And I guarantee there won't be anyone we know where we're going!"

"Promises, promises," I said, and then ducked as he made a playful grab for me.

Daniel was so sweet. Not at all like Dustin Roche. Yes, I was definitely making the right decision.

Not that Dustin was ever a consideration. I mean, we hated each other. From his elementary school taunts to his high school teasing, I resented him. Toward the end, just before I'd left town to pursue my career, Dustin could still get under my skin. I still remembered our last encounter.

"So, little Krista is heading off for the big-city lights, and maybe a big-city man?"

"That wouldn't be any of your business," I had told him.

"Everything you do is my business, little girl. Don't you know that?"

And on and on it would go. Yes, when I left home, I was genuinely relieved to be away from Dustin. I made a good start on that big-city career, too. Only, I'd made the mistake of coming home for a long visit last summer. That's when I met Daniel.

Daniel was new to town. He was just passing through on a trip around the world. It just so happened that Dustin's older brother, Tim, had been Daniel's best friend in college. Tim had died in a traffic accident several years ago; Daniel was just visiting with Tim's family when I met him.

I sure didn't want to fall in love with anyone from my hometown, and Daniel was a city guy, which suited me just fine. We would move into my small apartment in the city after we returned from our honeymoon. Daniel was in computer sales and he made a good living; I figured it wouldn't be long before we could find a bigger place and start a family.

My mom, of course, was worried that I hadn't known him for very long. "You know, Krista, I always hoped that . . . well, that you would marry someone from around here."

"Don't even say it, Mom! You hoped I'd marry Dustin—is that right? Well, I know a lot of people in town thought as much, but the truth is, we don't even like each other!"

"There's a thin line between love and hate, honey. Why, when I first met your father, I thought he was the rudest, most thoughtless young man on the face of the earth!"

That made me sit up and take notice. "Really? But, the two of you are so much in love—even today," I said, stunned.

"Yes, but it wasn't always that way, dear. Your father pestered me until I went out with him. He took me to the movies and talked nonstop; I couldn't even hear the movie! So, I dumped a large soda in his lap!"

"You didn't!"

"I most certainly did! And I thought that was the end of our 'relationship.' Boy, was I wrong!"

I had to laugh. My parents had this ongoing "argument" between them; they loved to disagree, and it was really funny to watch. My sisters and I all knew that they loved each other to distraction, but an outsider might think that they just didn't get along. But we could see through to the humor and love that made up their relationship.

I had to admit that my relationship with Daniel wasn't so subtle. What Daniel said was exactly what he meant; there was not even a smidgen of innuendo in him. Naturally, this made our love life very . . . straightforward. When Daniel was in the mood, he just said so.

With the wedding just a couple of days away, I had more than enough to keep me busy. The guests and my family would all be staying at the hotel, and the wedding would take place on the beach. There would be a large, white tent set up on the sand for the reception, and then everyone would go back to the hotel when it got dark so that we could dance into the wee hours. And then—the honeymoon in Mexico. I honestly would've been just as happy to just go back home to my little apartment and get to know Daniel with no distractions. But he insisted that I deserved a "real" honeymoon.

"Nothing but the best for my Krista!" he would say.

Sometimes, though, I honestly wondered how Daniel could afford all of this. After all, he'd just taken the past year off to travel the world. And now, we'd be honeymooning in Mexico and staying at one of the finest resorts in Cancun. Oh, I knew he made a decent wage. But, still—he hadn't worked in over a year! Nevertheless, I didn't want to spoil our romantic days by talking about money. I think many young brides must think like that.

It was inevitable that I had to bump into Dustin. So far, I'd managed to avoid him, but Daniel had hosted several parties for the family and our friends, and I realized that sooner or later, I would have to be civil to my childhood enemy.

"Krista," he said, giving me the once-over, "I wouldn't have recognized you."

"What's the matter, Dustin? Don't you have a bug or a snake handy to dump down the front of my dress?" I hissed, looking around to make sure that Daniel was on the other side of the room.

Dustin laughed. "Why should a bug have all the fun?" he asked with that devilish twinkle in his eyes—eyes that were fixed on the top button of my dress. I could see his fingers moving restlessly at his sides, just as though they were tempted.

I shook my head. Strange thoughts for an almost-married woman to have about the best man! I put it down to nerves about my wedding day, and all the talk I'd heard about the approaching hurricane. I realized I was just about ready to snap.

Suddenly, Dustin got serious. He guided me into a quiet corner and then went to get us both a glass of punch. When he returned, he asked in a low whisper, "You're all right with this? This is what you want, right?"

I stared at him. "No; I just spent thousands of dollars to bring my friends and family here just so they could see the hurricane together! What do you think?"

"It's not too late, you know."

"Not too late for what?"

He shrugged.

Ignore him, Krista. He's just trying to get to you—just like he always does.

But I was a grown woman now, and I knew a thing or two about life. I wasn't that little kid anymore, headed off to grade school, dreading that with each step, I might bump into that awful Dustin Roche.

So I stared him down. Dustin wasn't prepared for this maneuver; he gave me a slow salute with his punch glass and then disappeared into the crowd. The next time I saw him, he was talking to a blonde I didn't know. I went and caught up with Daniel and gave him a big kiss, to the oohs and aahs of our guests. I could only hope that Dustin had seen!

The good thing about a wedding is that you don't have time to think. We went through the rehearsal, and then the soon-to-be wedding party had a late supper. By then, I was exhausted and wanted nothing more than to sneak into my lonely hotel room and fall fast asleep.

"Not long now, darling," Daniel said. "Soon, we'll be waking up to each other for the rest of our lives."

I should have been thrilled by those words. I wanted to be, but I wasn't. Again, though, I put it down to being so tired. And I was still anxious about the weather. After all, we were having the ceremony and reception right on the beach, so the weather had better cooperate! A couple of the wedding guests had been listening to the forecast updates on The Weather Channel, but no one really knew for sure where and when the hurricane would hit land, much less how strong it would be if and when it did.

"I'll say a little prayer for you," my great-aunt June told me. "Everything will work out just fine in the end, dear."

Auntie June was something of a psychic in our family. She had these strange feelings that would often turn out to be premonitions of some kind. I wanted to ask her if she'd had any premonitions about my wedding day, but I was honestly afraid to ask.

The next morning I was rudely awakened by my sisters, who all told me that I'd overslept and that they'd arrived to get me ready for my wedding. I looked outside and the whole world looked gray, with strange-looking clouds in the sky.

"This doesn't look good," I mused aloud. "What does The Weather Channel say?"

My sisters looked at each other.

"Mom and Dad have just gone down to the beach to make sure everything's okay," Jan said.

"I'm sure it will be," Teri told me, sitting me down in front of the mirror so she could start my makeup.

All during the "bride-ification" process, I was feeling more and more claustrophobic. Honestly, it was like I just couldn't get enough air. So when they'd finally finished with me, I stepped out of the room.

"I'm just going to get a breath of fresh air. I'll be right back," I told them.

I knew that I couldn't go downstairs in my full wedding gown; I just wanted to be alone for a few minutes to gather my thoughts—my last thoughts as a single woman.

Dad had told me stories about this old hotel. He'd told me that he and some of the other busboys had used to sneak up to the roof to drink beers and horse around. So I got into the elevator on my floor and pressed the lighted, numbered button for the top floor, hoping that would mean the roof.

The elevator stopped on the floor above the one I was staying on. The doors slid open. Then, to my horror, Dustin Roche strutted into the elevator like some living nightmare from my childhood. He was carrying a tasty-looking Bloody Mary in a hurricane glass, complete with the requisite celery stalk.

"Not you!" I groaned.

"Yes, me. The one and only. And just where do you think you're going? If you want to escape, shouldn't you be going down? No— don't tell me—you're going up to the roof to jump, right? Why not just tell him no?"

I glared at him. For some reason, he was being particularly mean to me—on my wedding day, of all days. "I just wanted to be alone," I said pointedly, and stabbed again at the button for the roof.

"Doesn't sound too healthy to me—a bride who wants to be alone."

I sniffed the air. "You've been drinking! At this hour?"

"You think I've been drinking—you should've seen your groom! Not to mention every other man in the wedding party, with the possible exception of the minister. Jeez, Krista—this is a wedding, for Pete's sake! A celebration! Only, you don't look like you've got anything to celebrate."

"That's—"

"I know, I know. That's none of my business. Okay. So let's go on up to the roof. You can be alone in one corner, and I can have my Bloody Mary in another."

"Hair of the dog, huh?"

"Precisely. Plus, I'm a little stressed."

"Stressed? Why are you stressed?"

I didn't get an answer to that. All of a sudden, the lights went out and the elevator jerked to a shaky, shuddering stop. I squealed and instantly, Dustin's arms were around me.

"It's all right. Just a little power outage, is all. I'm sure we'll be on the move again real soon."

"Not soon enough for me," I said, glad that he couldn't see my frightened face in the dark. But I'm sure my voice was shaky.

"We must be at the roof now, anyway. I'll see if I can pry the doors open."

In the darkness, I heard him feeling around for the doors. He tried to pry them open with his bare hands, but they wouldn't budge.

I groaned. "What now?"

"We'll just have to sit tight and wait for the power to come back on. What are you so afraid of, anyway? That Daniel will find another bride in the next ten minutes?"

"Shut up!" I shouted, my nerves snapping. "Just shut up!"

There was a long silence in the dark elevator. Instantly, I was ashamed of my outburst. But why should I care what Dustin thought of me? Once I was married, I didn't plan on ever seeing him again. Daniel and I would be far away, happy together in the city.

Nevertheless, it seemed to be taking an awfully long time for the power to come back on. The silence was overwhelming. And then I could hear the wind, somewhere outside.

"It—it feels like we're on top of the roof," I said. If I was going to be trapped inside that elevator for a while with Dustin, it just didn't make sense not to talk.

"We are. Haven't you ever been up to the roof before?"

"My dad used to. He worked here when he was young."

"Me, too."

I didn't tell him that I already knew this. I didn't want him to think that I was interested in his life or anything he did. I heard another gust of wind and the elevator shook on its cables.

"We must be at the top. The elevator shaft ends in a little shack built onto the roof."

"Are you saying that we're sitting on the roof in a shack, with a hurricane on its way?" I asked, my voice rising.

"Yes, that's exactly what I'm saying. But I'm sure that someone will be missing one of us in the next few minutes. I mean, Daniel will be tearing this place apart, looking for you."

There seemed to be some kind of resentment in his voice when he said this last bit, and I wondered about that. He and Daniel were friends, after all. Then was it about me? Did Dustin hate me so much that he couldn't stand to see his best friend marrying me?

"Here," he said suddenly. "I've taken off my jacket. You can sit down on it. You'll be more comfortable."

"Thanks," I said, pushing my high-heeled sandals off gratefully. I felt my way down to a sitting position. I could feel the warmth of his body beside mine as Dustin tried to pry the doors open again without any luck.

"Isn't there a phone?" I asked.

"No. This is a really old elevator. It goes with the really old hotel."

Another gust of wind shook the elevator. It was getting cold. I felt the wind's cold touch on my face and instinctively, I shrank away from it.

"You're shaking. Are you cold?" Dustin asked.

I nodded, then remembered he couldn't see me. In the darkness of that elevator, we were just shadows to each other.

"The dress doesn't help," I said, pulling at the top of the strapless bodice.

"You've got that right; not much to keep you warm. Did Daniel pick it out?"

"Leave Daniel out of this, Dustin!"

"So it was your idea to look like a hooker on your wedding day?"

There was another awful silence. I just couldn't believe that he'd said such a nasty thing to me. At first, I wanted to hit him. Seconds later, though, I felt like crying. I was a bride-to-be, trapped inside an elevator on her wedding day. A hurricane was coming and I was locked in alone with the most hateful man on the face of the earth!

I started to cry. Normally, the toughest business meeting with the hardest-nosed client couldn't phase me a bit. But on my wedding day, with everything that had happened and my sudden, strange doubts about Daniel, it was all quite simply too much for me to bear.

It took Dustin a few moments to realize that I was crying. "Aw, Krista, I didn't mean that. . . ." he began.

"Yes, you did! Why would you say it if you didn't mean it?"

Hands reached for me, pulling me to my feet and close to his hard, warm chest. One hand drew my head against his chest; he was so gentle, like he was trying to take back his nasty words.

I allowed myself a good cry. There was some satisfaction in knowing that all of my makeup was running and ruining his expensive, white shirt. I pulled away after a moment, though, wondering what people would think when they finally rescued us.

We passed another half an hour or so in silence. Right about this time, I realized, everyone would be gathered on the beach, waiting for the ceremony to begin.

Why hadn't anyone come looking for me?

As though in answer, another big burst of wind shook the elevator.

"Well, you're going to get your wish; Daniel can't marry me if he doesn't even know where I am."

"Is that what you think? That I'm against you two marrying?"

"Isn't that the truth?" I challenged. I wished that I could see his face. As it was, I could faintly see him taking a step away from me in the close-quarter shadows.

"I just . . . I don't think you two are exactly right for each other. I mean, it seems like you hardly know each other."

"Maybe that's not a bad thing. After all, I know you very well, and. . . ."

"And what?"

But I didn't know the answer to that one. I was going to say that I hated him, but I realized, suddenly, that that wasn't true. Granted, he really got under my skin. But even that didn't explain the intensity of my feelings for Dustin. I just couldn't even explain it to myself, let alone to him.

"Never mind," I said, feeling deflated.

"Chicken," he said, laughing.

"Oh, Daniel, where are you?" I whispered to myself. But from the way Dustin stopped laughing suddenly, I knew that he'd heard me.

"Tell me the truth. Why were you headed up to the roof, anyway?" he asked suddenly. "Were you having second thoughts?"

"No. What about you? Why were you really going up there? You could've had a drink almost anywhere."

The wind had picked up outside so that now, there was a constant, unsettling whine all around us. Just then, we heard some wood snapping, too.

"What was that?" I asked.

"Probably just some stuff on the roof blowing around."

"How safe is this shack we're in?"

"Safe enough. And I'd imagine that the elevator shaft is pretty sturdy; it should hold. I mean, this old hotel has withstood more than a few of these storms."

Even though things were steadily getting worse outside, Dustin's calm voice settled my nerves. I had the crazy feeling that nothing bad could happen when he was with me—even though we couldn't stand each other.

"Don't worry, little girl; I won't let anything happen to you," he said softly, so low that I had to strain to hear him above the howling wind all around us.

"Where are they?" I asked after a few moments, nearly moaning with rising unease.

"Patience. You never did learn that, did you?"

"No. I've never seen any use in it," I shot back acidly.

"But I'm a patient man. And I think that now, all of my patience is finally about to pay off."

"What are you talking about?"

"Nothing. Nothing you would understand, anyway," he replied mysteriously.

He was right: I didn't have much patience—not about waiting for someone to decide to rescue us, and not about crazy talk from a man I didn't even really like.

"Try the door again," I said.

"It won't budge."

"Just please try it again, Dustin."

It was awful being stuck up there and not knowing what was going on in the rest of the hotel. If no one had come to get us yet, did that mean that the hotel had been evacuated because of the hurricane? Had we just been left behind to die, then? I couldn't believe that my parents would let it happen—that Daniel would let it happen! Or hadn't they guessed that I was still in the hotel? Maybe my mother thought I'd run off, jilted Daniel virtually at the altar. The way I'd run out on my sisters—likely with a look of panic on my face—it wasn't so far from the truth!

"Did you tell anyone that you were going up to the roof?" I asked Dustin.

"No. But you did, right?"

"No. No one knows I'm here."

"Maybe they think we ran off together, then."

It was meant to be a joke, but neither of us laughed. I realized that that would probably be exactly what Mom would think! After all, she'd always said that Dustin and I would get together someday. She was a hopeless romantic, and by now, I was sure she'd told other people what she suspected.

And Daniel. Poor Daniel! What would he be thinking right now?

"Well, we might as well get comfortable," Dustin said with a sigh. I could hear him settling himself down on the floor. I followed suit reluctantly.

"I wonder what time it is," I said.

"Do you really want to know?"

No, I really didn't. I didn't want to imagine everyone giving up on me ever showing up at my own wedding. I didn't want to imagine the hurt and fear in my parents' eyes. I might be missing, or I might have just bolted. They didn't know.

By now, there was a constant banging from somewhere outside. The wind had reached a steady scream and was only getting worse. Then, even worse, I could actually hear the waves crashing against the beach—maybe even against the hotel. I tried to swallow my panic.

"Why doesn't somebody come?" I asked. It was more of a whimper.

I felt a muscular arm encircle my shoulder and for once, I didn't care that it was Dustin's. Right then, I needed all the comforting I could get. I leaned against him.

I must've dozed a bit. When I woke up, the noise outside was worse, steadily worse. I clutched at Dustin's shirt and he rocked me back into an uneasy sleep.

I don't know how I would've survived that night without him. It was the worse night of my entire life—my wedding night, no less—and I think it must have been for Dustin, too. Still, guys aren't supposed to show their fear, and he didn't. He just held me protectively, giving me his warmth when the elevator turned into a freezer as night approached. He had a soft side, this man who I claimed not to like very much; he seemed to know just when to hold me. And he held me tighter when nature's fury would scream and shake our little enclosure up there on the roof. As much as it terrified me, I didn't really think that anything really bad could happen while I was with him.

But it might have been the last night of our lives, for all we knew. After all, no one can predict the damage a hurricane will do. Certainly, none of us in the wedding party had any idea about how bad it was going to get. Maybe thinking that there was a real chance that we could die made me say things I wouldn't have normally.

"Tell me the truth now," I told him quietly. I knew he was awake.

"Anything."

"Why don't you want me to marry Daniel?"

"Oh, we're back to that, are we?" He leaned over in the dark and kissed my temple lightly.

"I need to know, Dustin," I insisted.

"All right. I just—I think you deserve better, that's all. I mean, I know Daniel has told you the truth and you're all right with it and everything. I mean, you must be. Otherwise you wouldn't be marrying him."

"All right with what?" I asked, pulling away to stare at him in the gloom.

There was a long silence.

"He didn't tell you, did he, Krista?"

"Tell me what?" I demanded. I was running out of patience. When he didn't answer me, I reached for his hands to get his attention. "You tell me, Dustin. Since obviously, Daniel hasn't."

"I thought you knew. Honestly. He told me that he'd explained it all to you and that you said you would stick by him no matter what."

I was about to scream, a scream to match the fierce, high-pitched howling of the storm outside. At that point, I was truly frightened.

"Daniel's being investigated for fraud, Krista. Something to do with his last job. He's been trying to outrun the law through all that travel he's been doing, but they've finally caught up with him."

"Oh, my God," I whispered. All of my suspicions were real; it was a bride's worst nightmare.

My fiancé, guilty of fraud? I felt a stab of guilt then. He'd been accused, after all—not convicted. If I were truly his life partner, then shouldn't I at least give him the benefit of the doubt?

"I swear, Krista—I thought you were okay with this."

It must've been my day for crying, because I dissolved in tears again. First I'm trapped in an elevator in the middle of a hurricane, and now this. My bridegroom might be in jail right now, for all I know!

And the man who was comforting me, the man who took me into his arms, was not my Daniel. No, he'd left it to someone else to tell me the truth—or had he ever intended to tell me himself? Was I going to find out about it the day they dragged him away in handcuffs?

My sorrow turned to anger. How could he have kept this from me?

"I never want to see you suffer like this again, Krista. And if I have anything to do with it, you won't," Dustin said, rocking me gently as the wild wind howled all around us.

I felt numb. Even the storm could no longer scare me. I just waited for morning and the time when I would have to face Daniel again.

We spent almost twenty-four hours in that elevator before we were rescued. I blinked as the light of day finally entered our little prison and Dustin handed me over to a firefighter, our rescuer. Outside, the storm was easing. When we got down to the ground floor of the hotel, we could see that the sea had swept in. The elegant old carpets were soaked. In fact, the hotel had been evacuated just moments after I'd decided to go up to the roof.

Mom and Dad had thought that I'd been taken to a local community center that had been set up for refugees from the storm. When they couldn't find me there, they'd started frantically looking for any police officer or paramedic who would heed their predicament. Right about that time, it was discovered that Dustin was missing, too.

"I have to admit, the thought of you two running off to elope did cross my mind," my mother sheepishly told me later.

She'd tried to find Daniel again. But it seems that right around that time, people started to figure out that Dustin and I were missing— maybe even together—so then Daniel took off, too.

He hasn't been seen to this day.

I believe now that Daniel knew that Dustin would tell me about the fraud investigation, and that's why he left. I wish he could have been enough of a man to face me, at least one more time to explain himself. But the Daniels of this world really are cowards; I honestly don't think he would have ever told me the truth if he thought he wouldn't have to. I would have had to hear it from the police.

Thankfully, everyone was incredibly kind to me after all that had happened. No one even mentioned my almost-wedding. I went back to the city to try to pick up the pieces of my life. It was strange, though; after awhile, I hardly thought about Daniel at all. To this day, I consider myself a lucky woman because I didn't marry him.

But all that time, I was thinking of another man—a man who'd held me tight through the scariest night of my life. And then, out of the blue, I got a letter. Inside the envelope, I found a key chain with a tiny, brass life preserver on it.

Just in case you ever find yourself caught in another storm without your knight in shining armor. Dustin.

At the bottom of the note was his phone number.

I decided right then and there to find out if the boy with the snakes and frogs had finally grown up.

"It's me," I said, my hand shaking as I held the phone.

"Hello, Me." He laughed—that laugh I remembered all too well.

How long had I wanted him?

I was about to find out.

THE END

MY BIG, BEAUTIFUL WEDDING
Will tragedy ruin the day?

On my twenty-first birthday my longtime boyfriend, Jeremy, asked me to marry him.

"We've been together for six years now, Audrey," he said one balmy evening in June. "It's about time we get hitched."

Not the most romantic proposal, but it sounded great to me! I gave him a big kiss. "The answer is yes, in case you didn't already know!"

My parents were delighted; they were both very fond of Jeremy. "We'll have a Fourth of July engagement party!" my mother said merrily, beaming with joy. She loved parties.

"That's in just three weeks," Dad challenged. "Most places require reservations months in advance."

Mom gave him one of her silencing looks, her eyes narrowed into slits. "I wasn't planning on a restaurant or anything; after all, what's wrong with a backyard barbecue? And we do have a brand-new deck." We lived in a modest, two-bedroom, ranch-style home, but our backyard was fairly large.

"That could work," Dad conceded.

"What happens if it rains?"

That astute question came from my sister, Jenna, who is four years younger than I am. Always the practical one, she could put a pin in anyone's balloon.

Mom sighed. "She's got a point. It could rain and we don't have enough room in the house for everyone we'll want to invite."

That was putting it mildly. Our living room was crowded if more than six people were in it. Our kitchen was the biggest room, with a dining area to one side. That's where everyone always congregated whenever we had company, anyway.

"I have the perfect solution," Dad announced.

"What's that?" we all asked in unison.

He paused for dramatic effect. "Well, it just so happens that I have a contact for a large tent—one big enough for, shall we say, a hundred and fifty people."

It turned out that one of my father's close friends was a fireman with access to just such a tent. The problem was solved—even Jenna couldn't find fault.

My Fourth of July engagement party was one of the happiest occasions in my life. Jeremy gave me a beautiful, diamond engagement ring; it belonged to his grandmother and he had it reset for me with sapphires on each side of the one-carat stone.

That day turned out to be sunny and clear—not even a drizzle. Dad and several of his friends manned the charcoal grills, dishing out huge platters piled high with barbecued ribs, chicken, burgers, and hotdogs. Mom, an excellent organizer but a terrible cook, had ordered tons of potato salad, coleslaw, macaroni salad, soda, and beer.

"Oh, I can't wait to dance at your wedding!" Mom gushed to me later. "We'll go and see several bands before deciding on the one we want."

Jeremy and I were giving ourselves a year to plan for our wedding. As it was, I was entering my senior year of college, majoring in elementary education, and I would graduate in May. Our wedding date was set for the end of June.

Naturally, Mom immediately began the planning of this momentous occasion. "Audrey, I want you to have the best wedding ever! Your father and I have put aside money to help pay for it, so we should be able to have a splendid affair!"

I'd been working part-time as a salesclerk in a discount department store while attending college. "I can contribute something, too," I told her. "I've saved up a few thousand dollars already."

"Oh, Audrey, that's sweet of you to offer up your hard-earned savings, honey, but you'll need that money to furnish your first apartment. Besides, Dad and I feel it's our responsibility to see that you have a good sendoff into married life."

"With all of your connections, Mom, at least my wedding gown won't cost too much." Mom had worked as a saleswoman in an upscale dress shop since Jenna was in first grade. She always bought her good outfits from the sales rack, and with her employee's discount, their clothes were pretty reasonable. Whenever Jenna or I needed dressy stuff, Mom always took us to her shop.

"That's one place where we'll save," she agreed. "And don't forget—your father can save you guys a ton of money on your appliances."

Dad sold large appliances like washing machines and refrigerators at a store in town. With a basic salary and commissions, he did nicely.

Still, there were so many details to consider—choosing a location for the wedding reception, selecting a band, picking out the invitations; deciding on the menu, the photographer, the guest list. . . . After more than a month of searching, we finally discovered the ideal space—a private tennis club that had an enormous ballroom. A raised stage at one end could hold a large band.

"This is perfect," I said when we went for a tour, visualizing the whole scene in my mind. "And just look at those beautiful chandeliers and those long, French windows!"

"It's elegant," Mom agreed. "We can have the cocktail hour in the large entranceway and have tables set up in that long corridor outside the ballroom. We want your wedding to be absolutely wonderful, sweetheart—a day we'll all remember for years and years to come. It's the one special day in your life, darling—just remember that!"

Dad agreed with her, so who was I to question it? Occasionally, though, I'd think about the thousands of dollars my wedding was going to cost and wonder if Jeremy and I would be better off eloping. I figured we could certainly put all of that money toward a down payment on a house; that idea, I knew, was a good deal more practical than a lavish affair.

But then, I also knew, I'd be dashing my parents' dreams of seeing me walk down the aisle in a spectacular, white gown. As it was, Dad was really looking forward to giving me away, and Mom already had a mother-of-the-bride gown in mind for herself. They talked endlessly about how they'd dance the night away in that resplendent ballroom; in some ways, I realized, they were going to relish the event as if it were their own wedding.

"We never had a proper wedding," Mom told me. "Dad was in the Army at the time, and on one of his furloughs, we just went off together and got married by a justice of the peace. Your father took me out for a steak dinner afterward and that was the extent of our celebration."

The summer rolled along pleasantly, even though we were all very busy. I took a few summer classes and continued working at my part-time job. When I didn't have to work at night, Jeremy took me out for casual dinners—hamburgers or pizza, usually. We'd spend hours in Applebee's or Pizza Hut discussing our future together—where we wanted to live, the kinds of furniture we liked, and how many children we wanted.

"You do want a big family, don't you?" Jeremy asked me one evening at Applebee's over dessert.

"I'd like to have children," I answered carefully. "But not right away. I want us to have our own home first. Kids need room to play and run around and it's hard to give them that living in a small apartment."

"Maybe we won't have to wait a few years," Jeremy said with a knowing smile. "Some people will give us checks as wedding gifts and we might have enough for a down payment right away."

I shook my head. "You're being too optimistic."

"We'll see," he replied.

I thought about our conversation later, wondering, Does he know something I don't? Even if he did, I knew I wouldn't be able to worm it out of him. Jeremy can be pretty stubborn and close-mouthed at times.

Shortly after Thanksgiving, Dad came down with a bad cold that subsequently turned into the flu. He was out of work for a whole week, most unusual for him. The weeks between Thanksgiving and Christmas are the busiest ones in the retail business, and both of my parents always worked long hours during this time. Mom worked six days a week and two or three nights, in addition, and often she came home too exhausted to do anything but lay on the couch with her feet up on a cushion. Sometimes she was even too tired to eat dinner, so Dad usually picked up a pizza or Chinese takeout from Uncle Chang's on his way home.

I was busy with a full schedule of classes, working, and trying to spend some time with Jeremy, so I didn't really notice my parents' exhaustion at first. But then I began to realize that Dad never really recuperated from the flu; in fact, he seemed to be dragging himself from home to work and back again. By the time Christmas came, he was down once again with a sore throat and a high fever and Mom was worried about him. I could tell from her expression.

"Frank, you'd better see the doctor for a complete checkup. You're running yourself down," she told him one day.

"Don't worry, doll; I'll be fine. It's just a bad cold," he insisted. "Anyway, we're going to get away someplace warm next month, no matter what. We could both use a vacation."

Mom looked skeptical, but she didn't say anything while I was around. Later, though, I heard from Jenna that she and Dad had discussed going away and ultimately decided that they couldn't afford it that year. Jenna didn't have to tell me why they couldn't afford it—I knew why. And it made me feel horribly guilty.

Then again, it's their choice, I told myself. They're the ones who want me to have a big, lavish affair. Not that I don't want it. But I could certainly live without it.

Heavy snow and unusually cold temperatures ushered in a bitter winter. Dad came down with another severe cold in February and that time he finally agreed to get a complete checkup. As it was, he'd been having headaches for the past month and couldn't find any relief.

"I think I'm falling apart," he joked tiredly one night. "Oh, well; they say when you hit fifty, you're over the hill."

That week Dad had his checkup. The doctor gave him a complete physical and ordered several tests, including extensive blood work, just to rule out anything serious.

I knew something was wrong when I returned home from work that Friday night. My parents usually went out to dinner with friends every Friday, but that night they were at home, sitting on the couch when I walked in. It was very quiet in the house—the TV wasn't even on. Dad had his arm around Mom and they both looked worried.

"Hi," I said nervously. "I thought you two would be out to dinner."

"We don't feel up to it tonight," Mom said. Then she glanced at Dad and whispered something. I couldn't hear what she said, but he nodded. Then: "Audrey, sit down a moment, please, dear. We've had a call from the doctor."

Something in her tone of voice sent a cold chill running down my spine. I sat down opposite them and waited to hear the rest.

"Sweetheart, you know Dad's been having these terrific headaches lately."

I nodded, feeling my eyes fill with tears for what I somehow already knew was coming.

"It seems there's a small tumor in his brain that's pressing on a nerve, right behind his left ear."

She paused and it was so still in that room that you could've heard a pin drop. I could scarcely breathe.

"The doctor says an operation is necessary to remove it. There's a fifty-fifty chance that he could lose hearing in that ear."

She stopped speaking and I could see then that she was making a concerted effort to remain calm. Dad was ashen-faced; I'd never seen him looking so frightened before. In our family, he was always the strong one, always the rock we clung to in desperate or difficult times, always comforting us if we got hurt or were upset. This new aspect of him was very difficult for me to accept.

"Does Jenna know?" I finally asked in a voice that hardly sounded like mine.

Mom shook her head. "She was on her way to a party with Ethan tonight. We didn't want to spoil her evening. Tomorrow night, we'll tell her."

"When is the operation?"

"Dad has to see the surgeon next week. Then they'll set a date. Probably in a few weeks."

I couldn't help thinking about my upcoming wedding. Will this new turn of events affect that? I wondered.

I was afraid to ask.

The next few weeks were strange. Mom tried to maintain a "life as usual" attitude, but it didn't take a genius to sense her anxiety. Dad continued to work up until the operation date; in fact, he tried to get in as much overtime as possible, as his doctor had told him that he could plan on being out of work for at least six weeks.

Jenna was the only one who seemed unaffected and unfazed by Dad's situation. One evening, I finally challenged her about it. "Don't you even care what happens?" I asked. "You seem so caught up in your own little world—like Dad doesn't even matter!"

"Don't you lecture me, Audrey!" she snapped. "My God—what

do you want me to do? I keep busy and out of their hair—that's about all I can do."

Maybe she was right. But I couldn't take things so easily. I could see the strain it was putting on Mom; the dark circles around her eyes never went away, she wasn't sleeping well, and sometimes I'd hear her pacing the house at night. Once or twice I joined her in the kitchen in the early hours of the morning; I found her seated at the kitchen table drinking a cup of tea.

She was surprised to see me. "What are you doing up?"

"I could ask you the same question," I said, sitting down across from her at the table. "You're worried about Dad, aren't you?"

She sighed. "It'll be all right. The waiting's difficult, but once the operation is over we'll be back to normal."

Will we? I wondered about that.

The night before the operation Dad gave me a big hug and a kiss. I remember his eyes were full of tears; it was terrible seeing him so desolate. Mom was the strong one; she kept bolstering him up.

"It's going to be okay, Frank," she'd say. "We'll get through this; you'll see."

My parents seemed to have changed places. Dad had always been the strong one, as far back as I could remember. Now Mom was shouldering the whole burden, trying to keep everyone's spirits up and being the support for Dad to lean on.

Mom brought Dad to the hospital early the next morning. I'd arranged with Jenna to pick her up after school and we planned to keep Mom company through most of the long ordeal. The doctors had warned us that the operation could take several hours.

Driving to the hospital, Jenna was unusually quiet. "You doing okay?" I asked quietly.

She shrugged. "Yeah. I guess so. Audrey, can someone die from this operation?"

I looked over and saw the concern etched on her young face. "Anything can happen during an operation, but Dad has a good surgeon and I'm sure everything will be fine." I was determined to be optimistic—for her sake and for my own.

When we walked into the waiting room, Mom jumped up from her chair and came to greet us. "Dad's still in the operating room. The surgeon promised he'd see me as soon as it's over."

We sat down to keep her company. Suddenly, I wondered if she'd had anything to eat. "Mom, can I get you something from the cafeteria? A sandwich, maybe?"

She shook her head. "I'm not very hungry. Maybe a cup of tea, though."

I went down to the hospital cafeteria and hurried to pick it up.

Since I hadn't had lunch myself, I grabbed a tuna fish sandwich. I figured if Mom saw me eating, she might get an appetite. Always a slender person, she was really getting much too thin.

We sat together in that waiting room for almost three hours before the surgeon finally appeared. He looked pretty tired.

Mom was on her feet at the sight of him. "How's Frank, Doctor? Is he okay?"

"The operation went well. I was able to remove the whole tumor, but we'll have to wait and see how he recuperates."

"You don't know yet about his hearing, then?" Mom asked.

"No, not yet. I have to tell you, though, that in most cases, patients do lose their hearing."

At least he'd survived the operation. Jenna started to cry and I wrapped my arms around her. "It's okay, Jen," I soothed gently. "He's gonna make it."

Mom insisted that we drive home. She would wait and see Dad in the recovery room. "Don't stay too late," I cautioned her. "You need your rest, too, you know."

She gave me a wan smile. "I'll be all right."

Dad spent almost a week in the hospital. Mom visited him every day after work. The doctor's predictions were accurate—Dad did lose his hearing in that ear.

Jenna and I visited him most afternoons. We could see that he was very depressed. "Dad, you'll be fine soon," I told him, trying to cheer him up. "You're looking very chipper, in fact."

He gave me a sober stare. "Do you have any idea how much this is costing me? I'm losing six weeks of work—at least. And who knows if I'll even be able to return to my job without my hearing."

I hadn't thought about the financial consequences. I'd been concentrating on him just getting through the operation, but suddenly the whole impact of the situation hit me.

My upcoming wedding certainly isn't helping the situation, either, I realized.

That night I waited for Mom to get home from the hospital. I had a pot of tea on the stove for her, plus some blueberry muffins to tempt her appetite.

She looked thoroughly exhausted. "Thanks, Audrey; I could use a snack."

After she'd had her tea and a muffin, I offered to rub her feet.

She shook her head. "I'm just going to roll into bed. Thanks, anyway, sweetheart."

I followed her into her bedroom. "Mom, I don't want you and Dad to be under a financial strain because of my wedding. With Dad out of work, it's going to be hard for you, isn't it?"

She sat down heavily on the bed. "Audrey, we'll manage. You shouldn't be deprived of your wedding because of your father's illness. We're all looking forward to your special day."

And that was that. She was so adamant about it.

What else could I do?

Dad came home from the hospital on a Friday afternoon. He was out of work the whole month of April. Back at home, he moped around the house all day, watching TV or just staring into space. Mom bought him a complicated jigsaw puzzle to put together to keep him busy, but he couldn't concentrate on anything.

The time was drawing near to send out the wedding invitations. "Audrey, the invitations should be mailed the first week in May," Mom said one evening. She was sitting on the couch with her feet up on the coffee table, and that's when I noticed that one of her legs looked a little swollen.

"Is something wrong with your leg?" I sat down next to her.

"It's nothing—just from standing on my feet all day, that's all. Now, about the invitations. When you speak to Jeremy, tell him that we need a completed list of their guests by the end of April. I've already made arrangements with a calligrapher to do the addresses."

"Maybe you should take a few days off and rest your feet," I suggested.

"No. I'm better off working."

She didn't say why, but I gathered that staying at home with Dad could be a depressing experience—he was still so down most of the time. Also, there was the issue of money. Without my father's income, I knew that their finances were seriously strained.

Again, I offered to contribute the few thousand dollars I'd saved and again, the same response came back to me from Mom: "We'll manage without your money, sweetheart—keep it to buy furniture."

Dad went back to work in May and I breathed a sigh of relief. Now everything will get back to normal, I thought hopefully.

But he couldn't seem to shake off his depression.

"Why is Dad still feeling so low?" I finally asked Mom one day.

Instantly, Mom looked troubled. "He has this thing about being perfect. He was always in such great physical shape and now that he's lost the hearing in one ear, he feels . . . I guess the word for it would be, diminished. I just can't seem to get it through to him that he's okay and doing just fine."

"Do you think it would help if he saw a counselor?"

"I've suggested it, but he refuses. He doesn't believe that that's the answer. He says it will take time, that's all."

Final exams were coming up and I was busier than ever. Besides the wedding, I had my college graduation approaching. Still, I insisted that it wasn't necessary to fuss over it. With Jenna's high school graduation and my wedding, I felt that there was already enough fuss and certainly more than enough to do.

"But you're the first of our family to graduate from college!" Mom protested heartfully. "We should at least celebrate in some way—after all, it's a real accomplishment, sweetheart, and we're all so very proud of you!"

"Dinner at a nice restaurant is more than enough, Mom," I said firmly. "There's no need for another party."

By mid-May I was finished with school and I was elated. Now, I thought excitedly, I can focus completely on my wedding. There were final fittings for my gown and I had to select a veil and my shoes, and we still had to choose a photographer—we'd left it till the last moment and most were already booked for June.

Jeremy and I had discussed possible honeymoon trips. "Where would you like to go?" he'd asked me earlier in the year.

"Let's wait till spring and then decide," I'd responded. At the time, with so much happening in my family, the honeymoon was the least of my priorities.

Now, though, it was May and Jeremy insisted that we make plans. "In less than six weeks we'll be married, Audrey. We should make our reservations this week."

After everything I'd been through, I realized that it would be fun to get away for a bit; the past year had been hectic and difficult, to say the least. "How about a cruise?" I suggested.

"Fine with me. So where would you like to cruise to? The Caribbean? Alaska? There are so many places."

It didn't really make much difference to me, but I knew Jeremy wanted me to be specific. "How about the Bahamas?"

And so it was decided: We'd honeymoon on a cruise to the Bahamas.

Jeremy made reservations for a seven-day cruise, which necessitated a shopping trip to the mall on my behalf, as I realized I desperately needed some new, summery outfits for the trip. Mom and I usually shopped together so I asked her to come with me, and after searching through six different shops, I finally found a bathing suit that I liked.

"Good color for you," Mom remarked. She'd found a chair in a corner of the boutique and was sitting with her legs stretched out. She looked tired and I felt guilty for dragging her around all day from store to store.

"You just sit there and relax," I said. "I'll find some other things and try them on."

When we returned home, Mom made a beeline for the couch and

immediately propped her legs up on the coffee table with a labored groan.

"Want me to rub your feet?" I asked.

She smiled. "I'd love it."

For the next half-hour I massaged her legs and feet with a soothing, lavender lotion. "Jeez, your leg is pretty swollen, Mom," I said, frowning. "Does it hurt?"

She grimaced a little and nodded. "Sometimes. I made a doctor's appointment for Tuesday and he'd better give me something to bring down the swelling, because I am planning on dancing at your wedding no matter what."

I smiled. "Of course you will," I assured her. As it was, I couldn't imagine my parents not dancing at my wedding. They both kept telling me it would be one of the highlights of their lives.

Mom came back from that doctor with a prescription for a painkiller. "He says it's bursitis. He gave me a shot, so I should start to feel better soon."

Indeed, over the next few days she did seem to be recovering, and I was happy and relieved to think that that little problem had been solved.

Now if only we could revive Dad, we'd be in fine shape, I thought with a sigh. He was still deeply in the doldrums.

But when I talked to Mom about it, she made light of his moodiness. "Don't worry, Audrey—he'll perk up when he puts on his tux and walks you down the aisle. He's been waiting for that moment for years."

With less than three weeks to go, the excitement mounted. Mom's older sister was flying in from California and she hadn't seen her in several years. Dad's twin brother and his wife were also coming from a long distance away. Indeed, most of the RSVPs for the wedding were positive; more than two hundred guests planned to attend. At the last minute, we'd decided to invite children. Six of our "miniature" relatives would carry baskets of roses and scatter petals before them as they walked ahead of Dad and me down the aisle.

Everything moved along smoothly until sixteen days before the wedding.

Then the ground caved in under my feet.

I remember every single thing about that terrible day as if it were yesterday. In the morning, I left the house to interview for a teaching position in the fall. The interview went well; all of my credentials were in order and by the time I left the school, I had high hopes that I would get the position. In this optimistic mood, I drove to Jeremy's office to tell him about how pleased I was with my performance during the job interview. We planned to have lunch together before I reported to my part-time job.

Jeremy stood at the entranceway to his office as I pulled into the parking lot. He came toward my car when he spotted me, walking slowly, his usual cheerful expression replaced by a sorrowful grimness.

I exited my car and ran to him. "Jeremy, is something wrong?" A strange premonition had my heart pounding and my mouth was dry.

Without answering me, he gently but firmly took my arm and escorted me inside his office building. "Let's sit down first and then we'll talk," he said in a quiet, terribly calm voice.

His face was pale and drawn and I knew immediately that something terrible had happened; fear clutched at my throat as he led me inside, closed his office door, and then led me over to a chair. He knelt before me and took both of my hands in his before he spoke.

"Your father called about an hour ago, Audrey. He tried to reach you on your cell phone, but you must've been at the interview and had it turned off. That's when he called me." He paused and took a deep breath before he plunged ahead, firmly holding onto my hands. "It seems your mother wasn't feeling well this morning, Audrey, and she decided to stay home from work. Your father wanted to take her to the doctor's office, but she insisted that she'd be fine, that she only needed a day of rest. Her leg was bothering her again and she wanted to put cold compresses on it."

He paused and I jumped in. "How is she? Is everything all right? What's happened, Jeremy? What's going on? Please—just tell me!"

His face crumpled for a moment. Then he pulled himself together. "No, it's not all right, darling. Shortly after your father arrived at his job, your mother called him. She was having chest pains and difficulty breathing. Your dad called 911 to get emergency help and immediately drove home. By the time he got there, she'd collapsed, Audrey. The EMTs tried to revive her, but it was too late. She had a massive heart attack. Audrey, I'm so sorry."

This can't be happening—it has to be a nightmare, I thought. I started trembling, violently; all of a sudden I couldn't seem to catch my breath. Jeremy knelt in front of me and put his arms around my shuddering body as I started to wail and sob. He didn't say another word as tears ran down his cheeks.

"No!" I screamed, trying to push him away even though he wouldn't let me. "It can't be true! I saw her this morning! She gave me a hug and a kiss! She was fine! She can't be gone—she can't be. . . ." I couldn't believe what I was hearing.

My mother is only forty-nine years old! I thought with devastating anguish as my mind reeled. She can't be dead—she's too young to die!

Denial was my first defense. When that didn't work, I tried to numb myself. Zombie-like, I sat there with my mind a blank. But my body knew and it shook and convulsed with shock and horror.

"Audrey, honey, I'm going to drive you home now," Jeremy told me gently as he helped me to my feet. "Your father and Jenna need you now, Audrey. Try to pull yourself together, sweetheart."

Pull myself together? I thought. I haven't yet begun to fall apart. I was ice-cold and nothing seemed to register as I got to my feet. Jeremy walked with me to my car and drove me home.

Jenna came to the door when she heard us pull up in the driveway. Her eyes were red and swollen and Dad was right behind her, looking as white as a sheet.

I stumbled into the house, and it was only when Jenna put her arms around me that I really broke down. Huge, gulping, anguished sobs shook me as I realized the extent of our loss.

Mom has been my best friend and confidante all these years, I thought. How can I ever go on without her?

The house was thick with emotion as we all sat together in the living room, trying to make sense of that terrible tragedy. "I begged her to go to the doctor," Dad kept repeating over and over again. "But you know your mother; when she makes up her mind about something, her mind's made up." He started to weep and Jenna and I both rushed to embrace him.

He was right; Mom could be as stubborn as a mule—especially when it concerned her family's welfare. I realized suddenly and wrenchingly that she didn't want to upset all of our plans by becoming ill, so she'd tried to dismiss her symptoms, thinking that her pains would soon pass. I realized that that whole past year, Mom had been trying to get us "back to normal." At the very end, she couldn't face the idea of everything coming apart again, as it had when Dad was ill.

It's Dad's illness that dragged her down. As soon as I thought that wretched thought, a sudden jolt of anger rushed through me. If it weren't for his constant complaining and depression, Mom would still be alive!

Afraid to give voice to my fury, I retreated to my room and threw myself on my bed and sobbed my heart out. Jenna came in to see if I wanted a glass of water—a cup of tea. I didn't want anything. The only thing I wanted—my mother—was gone forever.

Jeremy came in and sat next to me and tried to soothe me. "Audrey, I know you're hurting, but we have some decisions to make about the funeral and notifying everyone . . . and about the wedding, too."

I cringed when he said it. The wedding! Who cares about a wedding? How can I possibly get married without my mother there to see me walk down the aisle? My mother and father were supposed to dance the night away at my reception!

Now, none of that would happen.

"I-I c-can't g-go th-through with it!" I sobbed. "I-I j-just c-can't!"

Then all of my anger, heartbreak, and bitterness poured out of me. Fortunately, Jeremy had closed the door when he came in. Wisely, he didn't interrupt; he let me vent my anger and sorrow as, for well over an hour, I wept and raged at destiny. From anger with my father, I turned on myself, thinking wildly, If I hadn't wanted this big, ridiculous wedding, Mom would still be alive!

"We should have eloped!" I wailed to Jeremy. "It was too much pressure for her! Oh, dear God—my poor, sweet, precious mother!"

Finally, the tears subsided; I could breathe normally again. Jeremy handed me some tissues and gently smoothed my hair. "It's okay, Audrey," he said softly. "It's really okay."

After awhile he began talking to me in a low, soothing tone of voice. "Just try to pull yourself together, honey. Jenna and your father need you now. Arrangements have to be made and you must help them. I know you can do it, Audrey—I just know you can."

With his support and encouragement, I rejoined my family for the sorrowful task of organizing my mother's funeral. Aunt Liza, Mom's older sister, flew in the next day from California. She was a reservoir of strength for all of us, helping with phone calls and the church service arrangements.

If it hadn't been for my fiancé's unfailing love and support, I could not have made it through. Jeremy never left my side, and his parents were equally helpful, lending a hand whenever and wherever necessary.

I still wasn't sure that I could go through with our wedding plans. How can I possibly pretend to be happy on that day? I wondered, and every time I thought about it, I would start to cry.

Jeremy didn't know what to say to me or what to do about the situation, but his expression was grave whenever the subject came up. I knew that I ought to consider his feelings in the matter, but I truly wondered how I could ever possibly go ahead with the most important event of my life without my mother by my side. Mom and I had worked together for a year planning the affair; every single aspect of my big day had been discussed and decided upon with her input. And now she would never be able to enjoy the fruits of her devoted labor.

It's not fair, I thought, absolutely heartbroken. It just isn't fair.

Jeremy waited until after the funeral to sit me down for a serious talk. "We need to work this out now, Audrey," he began gently. "Our wedding is less than two weeks away."

I immediately started to cry, feeling absolutely overwhelmed and overcome. "But I don't know what to do!" I sobbed.

"Just think for a minute, honey, about what your mom would want. She never canceled happy occasions, remember? No matter

69

what, she always forged ahead. That's why I know in my heart, Aud, that she would want us to go ahead with our plans."

I listened to him and, deep down, in the end, I knew that he was right; Mom would be the first one to say, "Go ahead. Have your special day, no matter what, Audrey. After all, it's what we planned all along."

Mom always had such spunk, courage, and determination, I remembered tenderly as Jeremy held me close. The least I can do is endeavor to emulate her for the rest of my life.

"Okay, then," I said to my fiancé when I had my composure. "I'll try to make it a happy occasion—I really will try."

My wedding day dawned clear and sunny. I could not have asked for better weather.

As far as the wedding itself, to be perfectly honest, most of it is a blur. The one thing that stands out is when my father walked me down the aisle. Though still gaunt from his recent illness and Mom's death, he looked so handsome in his new tux. I could see Jeremy waiting at the altar for me.

In that slow procession, with throngs of family and friends on either side, I had this clear vision of my mother watching it all from above. Her presence was so strong; I could hear her voice and see her face. She was smiling and I knew that she was happy. She may have been physically absent, but she was there for me, strong and loving, in my heart, always.

A year after her death, I find myself still talking to her, telling her about all that has happened. Usually I'm in my car driving to work and I'll start a conversation. I hear her answers, loud and clear.

She was the first one to know that I got that teaching job I interviewed for on the day she died. And when I found out that I was pregnant, I confided the news to her, too, first and foremost.

There's still some sadness. Now and again, I realize that she won't be able to play with her grandchildren—that she'll never babysit for them or see them grow up. Slowly, I'm gaining the understanding that I was very blessed to have her for all of my growing-up years. Nothing and no one can ever take that away from me.

And now I am blessed with a wonderful husband and super in-laws. They've welcomed me into their family with open arms, and Jeremy and I are expecting twins in a few months—a boy and a girl. We're going to name our little girl, Madeleine, after my mother.

Life truly does go on.

THE END

AM I GOOD ENOUGH
TO MARRY HER?
After all I've been through, I just want to
be worthy of the woman I love

I never thought this day would come.

Never in a million years.

I mean, even if I were the kind of man who's focused enough to have a plan—

I'm sure it wouldn't have included getting married.

It's two o'clock in the morning, a full eight hours until my wedding.

Ten o'clock is coming at me like a freight train and there's not a damned thing I can do to stop it.

I don't mind telling you that I'm scared to death.

I'm not afraid for me, but for my beautiful Rachel.

I pray to God that I will never let her down and that she will never come to regret her decision to spend the rest of her life with me.

Rachel likes to say that love can move mountains.

I hope she's right, because I've got a pile of issues the size of Eagle Mountain built up inside of me.

They're all coming to the surface tonight, as I sit here in front of the window, watching the snow drift down from the sky. It's deceiving, the way snow changes things. It covers all of the ugliness, but underneath, it's all still there.

I want to believe that Rachel's love has changed me . . . that underneath the decency and kindness she covers me with, I'm not still the same, aching welt of a man I was the day I met her.

I want to believe that I've left that man behind.

When I met Rachel I was just another poor slob trying to earn a living down at Harding Lighting Company. Like any factory, Harding is always hotter than hell, and just about as pleasant. I don't mind the work, so much as the heat. But it's not like I had anyplace better to be, and working was a way to escape myself until I could get my next cold six-pack, and when I got really lucky—a warm body to lay down beside me for a while.

That's how this whole thing started—

When Rachel came to work at Harding.

I'm not saying it was love at first sight. I've never believed in that kind of love—or any kind at all, for that matter.

Love has never come easy for me.

I grew up in a small, cramped apartment with three older brothers and a tired-out icicle of a woman who called herself our mother. Wayne was fifteen when I was born and John was twelve and Robby, eleven. I guess by the time I came along, Mom had already spent all of her tenderness on them. I tried for a long time to squeeze some maternal instinct out of her, tried to make her love me. But deep down, I always knew she never really wanted me in the first place. Knowing that hurt me for a long time, but after awhile, I just didn't care anymore.

I don't think my mother knew about the hell my brothers put me through. If she did, she didn't care. I left home the day I turned seventeen. I didn't say good-bye and I never looked back.

That was ten years ago.

I think about my mother, sometimes, and wonder if she's even noticed that I'm gone.

Up until now, the closest I ever came to love was a summer fling I had with a girl named Vanessa. She was cute, but not very smart, and I guess looking after her gave me a purpose in life. Vanessa was sweet and shy and she's the first person in my life who treated me like I was somebody. But like every good thing that comes my way, I lost Vanessa, too.

Three months into our romance I got Vanessa pregnant. I was eighteen, young, and stupid enough to believe that I was invincible. I wanted to support Vanessa and our kid, but her father had other ideas. He packed her off to Wisconsin one night and after that it was like I didn't even exist anymore. All of a sudden my girl had someone named Aunt Claudette to look after her and I wasn't even allowed to know where she lived.

I'm not saying she wasn't better off. She sent me a picture after Christopher was born and I could see a big, beautiful house in the background. I couldn't give Vanessa a house like that in a millennium. I knew that, even then. But what got me was that she didn't even love me enough to let me try.

Christopher's a cute kid. He has a fuzzy, blond head of hair and big, blue eyes and a smile that just sort of reaches out and grabs hold of a person's heart. I slept with his picture under my pillow for a long, long time. I'd take it out at night sometimes and stare at it, and it hurt me a lot that I couldn't be a father to him. I promised myself that if I ever got past the pain of loving Christopher, I'd never go back there again.

Christopher is eight years old now, but in my mind, he's still the baby in that photograph. I still take it out and look at it, sometimes, but it doesn't hurt me anymore.

People think I'm a coldhearted S.O.B., but I don't worry about it.

I feel things as much as anybody; I just don't show it. Maybe it's got something to do with the fact that I came up empty-handed every time I ever reached out to anyone. Or maybe it's all just backwash from the spinning game.

I don't really know.

When Rachel came into my life I felt my guard start to slip and that scared me. That's the reason why I was cold to her, at first. That's just the way it was with me—

The more I wanted something, the more I hated it.

Rachel is quiet. I don't mean just her tone of voice, or that soft, southern way she has of talking. Her quietness is more like an aura— like some sort of halcyon cloud she walks around in. It's like she lives in this calm, beautiful world that nobody else can see. In the noise and the ugliness of a place like Harding, that made her stand out like a neon sign.

The first thing that got my attention was Rachel's hair. It's a soft, reddish-brown color that reminds me of the jar of pennies I used to keep hidden under my bed when I was a kid. Rachel never wears any makeup. Most of the girls at the factory come to work buried underneath so much paint that you can't tell whether they're really pretty or not. Rachel looks natural—like the kind of girl who spends her time growing herbs and picking wildflowers. She's very childlike, and at Harding, we put a premium on anything that looks like innocence.

The foreman stuck Rachel on my line, her first night there. I showed her how to pack the light bulbs into the crates when they come down the conveyor belt and beyond that, I didn't talk to her. I watched her, though. From the corner of my eye I watched every move she made and believe me—I'm not the only one. You'd have thought she was a new selection in the vending machine, the way the slobs in my department salivated over her.

Oh, man, I thought, this chick is gonna be lunchmeat.

Right away I started feeling tense and nervous, like I needed to protect her. It was Vanessa all over again and I knew right then and there that I was in trouble.

After that night, Rachel sat with me every night on break, whether she was working my line or not. I'd be in the lunchroom, reading the newspaper, and I'd know without even looking when Rachel came in. It sounds crazy, but I could feel her happiness brightening up the room. She'd set her blueberry muffin and her carton of two-percent milk on my table and just sit right down. She never asked first, and what would I have said? Thanks for wanting to sit with me, babe, but I'd rather you just went away?

Even I'm not that cold.

73

Rachel was always reading poetry books. We'd sit without talking, Rachel with her book and me with my newspaper like some sort of old, married couple—except that I'd end up reading the same line for half an hour. And I seriously doubt that any man who's been with the same woman for any length of time can feel the agony I did, just sitting at the same table with Rachel. Half the time I just wanted her to leave me alone.

But then she did.

And that made it even worse.

Maybe she caught some bad mojo off me or maybe she just got tired of being ignored.

After a couple of weeks she started sitting with this dude named Jess. He's a goofy-looking kid—a real choirboy. I'd watch Rachel talking to him and try to figure out what the attraction was. I told myself that I didn't care, but the churning in my gut said I did care.

It said I cared a lot.

Then the schedules shifted around and one night Rachel ended up on my line again. I was nervous and edgy and self-conscious as hell. You'd never have known that, though.

I was as cold as an ice jam.

It was a bear of a job and halfway through it, my line went down. It took the rest of the shift and every swear word I know to get it up and running again. My foreman, Ed Briggs, came out at fifteen minutes before ten and told me the job was a priority. I'd worked at Harding long enough to know that that meant Rachel and I weren't going anywhere anytime soon.

The motor kept kicking off and by eleven the job still wasn't out. I was hot and frustrated and getting pretty tense. After about the fiftieth adjustment to my machine and the hundredth case of chewed-up light bulbs, I slammed my fist into the stop button. Rachel just stood there, looking at me like I was the man in the moon. I walked past her and muttered that I was going to get some coffee.

I didn't think she'd follow me. I went to the lunchroom, grabbed a cup of coffee, and sat down. I was drumming my fingertips on the table, ticked off at the world and trying to get a hold of myself, when Rachel walked in. She sat down across from me and just stared at me without saying anything. I opened the newspaper, but I couldn't concentrate on it. I could feel Rachel's eyes all over me and when I finally looked up again, she was resting her chin in her hands, staring straight at me.

"What?" I asked.

"What is it with you, Mike?"

"What do you mean?"

She kept looking at me with those beautiful eyes of hers, like she was trying to figure me out. "You're so full of anger. Is it all of life you hate, or just me?"

I didn't answer her; I just finished my coffee and walked out.

After a few more adjustments I finally got the line running smoothly again, but I couldn't feel good about it. What Rachel said kept chewing away at me. I know most people don't like me, and as I said before, I normally don't worry about it. But that time I was worried. Rachel thought I was the biggest jerk known to mankind and for some reason that bothered me.

It was almost one in the morning before the job was done. Rachel taped up the last skid of bulbs while I made out my paperwork. She didn't say another word and neither did I.

She was getting into her car when I walked through the parking lot. I started to walk past her, but then something made me stop. I didn't have a clue as to what I intended to say, so I jammed my hands in my pockets and just said the first thing that popped into my head.

"I don't hate you, Rachel."

She has this way of smiling. . . . Her smile starts in her eyes and spreads out across her face like a sunrise. "I'm really glad to hear that, Mike."

I gave her the closest thing I had to a smile and told her that I was thinking about going out and grabbing a beer.

We went to a bar called Jake's, out on Railroad Street. We sat down in a booth and right away, Rachel started talking. I found out that she's from Missouri and that she studied music at a college in Kansas City. She told me that she was a songwriter and then, finally, I felt like we had some common ground.

Don't get me wrong—I've never been to college and I've never seriously studied one damned thing in my life. But I'm a songwriter, too. I like to put my feelings down on paper and set them to music because they drive me a little less crazy that way. So we talked about music for a while, and then I asked her what she was doing in Minnesota.

"I don't know," she said, shrugging. "Just taking a little breather, I guess."

I couldn't quite figure that one out. I mean, who would come five hundred miles to work in a low-paying, roach-infested hole like Harding Lighting for no good reason?

I drank a lot of beer that night. I let Nels, the bartender, keep refilling our pitcher because I didn't want the night to end. But all too soon it was two o'clock and Jake's was closing for the night.

I stumbled out to my car and then Rachel put her hand on my arm. "Mikey," she said, "maybe you'd better let me give you a ride home."

We pulled up in front of my apartment and I still didn't want to let her go. I kept asking her questions about herself. Finally she said it was my turn, so I started telling her about my screwed-up childhood. I only meant to tell her a little, but instead I sat there and spilled the whole story. I even told her about my brothers, and about the spinning game. It might've been because she was sitting so close to me, or because she was looking at me with those incredible eyes, acting like she actually cared. Or maybe it was the beer.

We ended up talking all night.

Things changed between us, after that.

We started spending a lot of time together and like I said— Rachel's goodness just sort of wore off on me. I stopped drinking so much and I started to feel better about my life. By September I was even almost ready to admit that I was in love with her.

She was the best friend I'd ever had and I wanted so much more and it was killing me. I mean, there was Rachel, so beautiful and warm, and there I was, feeling all kinds of emotions that I never even knew I was capable of—and I never touched her. I wanted to so badly that it nearly drove me insane, but I didn't give in to the temptation. I was afraid that if I tried to take it to a sexual level, I'd lose what we had together, whatever it was. So I didn't. I didn't touch her. But God Almighty, I wanted to.

Then Labor Day was coming and I knew our time was running out. We didn't talk about it, but I knew that sooner or later Rachel was going to be leaving to go back to college. I started waking up at night in a cold sweat, worrying, but I could never bring myself to put my worries into words because if she was leaving, I couldn't bear to know.

Then September came and went and Rachel stayed in Minnesota and I started to breathe a whole lot easier.

We wrote a lot of songs together and Rachel asked me if I would mind if she sang some of them at her church. She knew that I didn't believe in God and she never asked me to go to church with her, and that was good for both of us. But she always told me about the services and after awhile my curiosity was killing me, so one Sunday morning I got in my car and drove over to her church.

The minute I walked in people started touching me—hugs, handshakes—all that. I don't like to be touched—especially by men—and I wasn't all that keen on being there in the first place, but I sucked it up because I wanted to see my girl do her thing. That's how I'd started thinking of Rachel, by then—as my girl.

She walked up to the front of the church and sat down on a stool with her guitar. She had on a white dress and the sun streamed in through the stained-glass windows, making her copper-colored hair glow like fire. She looked just like I've always pictured an angel would look. And then she started to sing, and I'd never experienced anything so incredibly moving. The song was about forgiveness, but somehow, it didn't sound the same as when we wrote it together.

That's when I got it.

That's when I finally knew what Rachel's all about.

I've known a lot of people who consider themselves to be religious. I've seen a lot of intolerance and a whole lot of misery inflicted in the name of religion and I never wanted any part of it. But that Sunday, as I thought about Rachel and the quiet way she lived her life, I started to think, Maybe there's something to it, after all.

After church we picked up some sandwiches from the supermarket deli and drove out to a nearby park. We hiked the trails for a bit, enjoying the autumn foliage. We sat down at a picnic area and ate our lunch and that's when Rachel laid it all out for me. She told me about God's love and the way she explained it, it seemed like the most natural, beautiful thing in the world. For the first time since I was a kid I really thought about God and how great it would feel to believe that He actually gives a darn. Then I started to get that familiar, aching feeling in my gut—that sickening sensation that I was spinning—and a cynical little voice inside my head told me it was all just a fairytale.

"I don't believe in that crap, Rach," I told her. "I'm sorry if that makes you mad, but I don't want any part of it."

"Okay, Mike," she said softly.

She didn't try to jam her religion down my throat, like a lot of people had in the past. She just said that someday she hoped I'd be able to accept God's love, and that I'd let Him help me work through my "frozen emotions."

I don't mind telling you—

That conversation hurt.

By Christmastime, just when I was feeling secure in our relationship, Rachel dropped a bomb on me. We were out walking and it was snowing so hard that you could hardly see two feet in front of you.

Rachel loves the snow, but she never quite got used to the cold. She was shivering like crazy, so I pulled her close to me. I was only going to try to warm her up a little bit, but then I started kissing her. We stood there in the snow and I just kept kissing her and softly murmuring her name. It was like twenty-seven years of wanting all crammed into one moment; I wanted so badly to tell her that I loved her, but somehow, I just couldn't get the words out.

Then all at once Rachel was crying.

"What's wrong, Rach?" I asked.

She turned away from me.

"Hey." I gently turned her to face me again and took her face in my hands. "Why won't you look at me?"

77

"I'm leaving after the first of the year, Mike. I'm going back to college."

Just like that. Bam! I went numb, and it had nothing to do with the frigid Minnesota afternoon.

"Can't you stay out a semester?"

"I've already lost a whole semester, Mikey. I feel it's time I move on."

"I don't want you to go, Rach."

She stood there crying, saying I'd be fine, we'd both be fine. I guess I panicked; I started grasping at straws—at anything that seemed like it might support the slim hope that I could somehow make her change her mind.

"You could transfer to a school here in Minnesota, couldn't you?"

She looked me square in the eye and asked, "Why would I do that, Mike?"

That killed me.

That one just about killed me.

I mean, here I'd wasted half a year trying to learn how to thaw out and be someone whom Rachel could halfway love. I'd stopped drinking. I'd gone to church and I'd gone without sex until it nearly drove me insane and it was all for her. All of it. Nobody was making her leave and if she didn't know by then why she ought to stay, then I sure as heck wasn't going to spell it out for her.

I dropped her hand. "Maybe you shouldn't," I said.

Then and there—I felt my heart turn back into a block of ice.

It ate away at me all that night. I tried to sleep, but when I closed my eyes I kept feeling myself start to spin. Rachel really had me going, I thought miserably. I walked right up to the edge, this time. I tied my own hands and all but begged her to give me a shove.

I avoided Rachel all that week. I guess in my mind she was already gone and I was trying to get used to the idea. Gosh, though . . . being without Rachel is almost like oxygen deprivation.

I started drinking again and one night I even went down to Jake's and picked up a girl. She was cheap and rough and afterward, I hated her.

But not as badly as I hated myself.

Rachel left Minnesota on the second of January. She knocked on my door on Christmas Eve, but I didn't answer. When I went out later, I found that she'd left me her Bible, and a note that read:

Mike, I hope that someday you will be able to believe in God's love. I will be leaving Minnesota on the second of the month. If you want to talk, you know my number. I will miss you and think of you often.

Love, Rachel

I know now that she was giving me one last chance to change her mind, but I was too dumb to see that at the time. I threw her letter in the garbage and shoved the Bible in a drawer along with all of the foolish notions I'd had of starting a new life with Rachel.

Rachel wasn't gone for even a week and I was a mess. I couldn't eat, couldn't sleep, and I couldn't even go to work because she wasn't there to make it bearable. My days were endless and my nights were pure hell.

I dialed her apartment every day. I guess some illogical little part of me was hoping she'd pick up the phone and the whole nightmare would go away. After about three days of calling, though, I finally got a cold, mechanical voice telling me that the line had been disconnected.

That's when I lost it. I thought about everything that was ever taken from me and everything I never had in the first place and all the things I never was and never would be. I thought about how sick I was of myself, and of being such a loser.

I thought about ending it all right there.

I got out the Bible Rachel gave me for Christmas and I started reading all of the verses she'd carefully outlined for me with a highlighter—verses about God's love, and how it makes a person new. With absolutely nothing left to lose, I got down on my knees beside my bed and for the first time in my life, I prayed. I didn't hear any heavenly chorus or feel the brush of angel wings, but the empty feeling inside of me eased and I knew then, somehow, that God heard my prayer. I also knew that if I let Rachel slip through my hands, I'd be the biggest fool who ever lived.

I loved that girl, and I got in my car and drove all night to tell her so.

I was a pretty sorry sight by the time I got to Kansas City. I stood outside the music building at her college and waited for her to show up. It was raining in Missouri, and I didn't even have a coat. Worse than that, I didn't have a plan.

I was leaning against the side of the building when finally, Rachel came out. She walked over and stood in front of me. She didn't ask what I was doing there; I guess the look on my face told her everything she needed to know. I felt my lip start to tremble and I stared down at my shoes.

"I'm not fine, Rach," I said. "You said I would be, but I'm not." She didn't answer, so I reached for her hand. "I want you to come back to Minnesota. Or I'll come here."

"Why would you do that, Mike?" she asked softly.

There it was again. Her gentle invitation to bare my soul. She might as well have asked me to strip off my clothes and stand there naked in front of her.

There's a little boy who's still buried somewhere deep inside of me. He wants to trust, but he's afraid. Standing there with Rachel, I felt that little boy start to tremble. He braced himself, getting ready for the game. . . .

My brothers used to blindfold me.

My mother was a nurse's aide who worked the nightshift at Mason Memorial. As soon as she left for her shift my brothers would get me out of bed. They'd tie a blindfold over my eyes and then Wayne would get the rusted, old coffee can from out of the closet. Inside the can were scraps of paper and on each paper, there was the name of a different "game." I don't know which one of my brothers made up the games, but every one of them was cruel and pitiless and degrading.

Worst of all was the spinning game.

The basement of our apartment building was cold and dark and it smelled like urine and dirty socks. In the corner of the basement there was a shower. My brothers would carry me, kicking and screaming, down the basement stairs. They'd tie my hands together and string me up over the shower rod and let the water run until it was good and cold.

God, I can still feel myself turning in the air, waiting for the pain. I can feel the icy water on my body and hear the snap of wet towels laying into my skin. Mostly, I can feel the darkness, and the eerie, terrifying quiet of waiting, after their footsteps pounded back up the basement stairs. Sometimes they'd leave me there for hours, spinning . . . naked . . . blindfolded.

It was usually John who cut me down.

"Don't you cry, little man!"

He always told me he was doing me a favor—toughening me up, getting me ready for the real world.

"This world belongs to the strong, little brother," John would say. "You show 'em you're weak, they'll chew you up and spit you out. You might as well learn that right now."

At four years old, I didn't understand it, but I never cried again.

Not until that morning in Kansas City with Rachel.

I took a deep breath. "Because I love you, Rach. Because I want you to be my wife."

I don't really know what happened to me, then. I started shaking all over, and this sound was coming out of my throat that was half a scream and half a moan. And then that little boy inside of me was crying. I mean—head in my hands, honest-to-God sobbing. And he couldn't stop. My shoes were getting wet; rain was dripping off my shirt and I was standing in a puddle of water and tears and twenty-seven years of loneliness and hurting.

And then Rachel's shoes were next to mine. I felt her arms wrap around me and if I had a million-and-one words at my disposal, I still could not describe to you even now the look that was in her eyes then.

Rachel healed me, that day.

Her love made me a better man.

But tonight, that ugly person I used to be comes back to haunt me.

He screams in my ear, reminding me that I was never going to let anyone get close, never going to let anyone in. He rejects Rachel's love like it's an organ transplant because he's too cold and too ornery and too damned stupid to see how very much he needs it.

There is a picture of Rachel sitting on the table in front of me. She's looking at me with those eyes of hers—eyes that say she is trusting me to be man enough to handle this. Beside the picture sits the Bible she gave me for Christmas.

I flip open the cover and I look at a picture of Jesus, walking on the water. He's looking at me, and I'm looking at Him, and I know I still have a long, long way to go before I'll qualify for anything even remotely close to sainthood. But then I look into Rachel's eyes again, and I've just gotta smile.

I don't know a lot about God, but I think of all I'm getting in a wife whom I could never even begin to deserve, and I know that He must love me a heck of a lot.

THE END

OUR WEDDING
WAS DEADLY

T ragedy struck on my wedding night. I must be the only man in the world who has had to bear the agony of watching my wife die slowly—her beautiful body contorted with pain, writhing tortuously in my arms. And to think those only moments earlier, she had been glowing with happiness and passion! Just a few seconds: that's all it took to steal the sunshine from my days and to engulf me in depressing darkness. How can I pick up the pieces of my life when I know for a fact that without ever having laid a finger on her, I unintentionally murdered the woman I loved?

Chae was my soul mate. I remember the way my heart swelled with happiness when I thought I had a lifetime to get to know this amazing woman, to discover her sweetness, and to explore her hidden treasures. But ours was not a fairy tale romance. It was far from it, in fact, because I had made one lousy Prince Charming.

Our relationship began in the spring of 2000, the historic turn of the century. I was a graduate student majoring in international finance at a top university. The future seemed promising. I was on top of the world. Footloose and fancy free, I had lived life in the fast lane for some time. Success, like an invigorating drug, went to my head. I dated a different girl every day of the week. Flashy cars, wild parties, and late nights . . . the entire scenario soon got sickening. I longed to settle down, to find some degree of companionship, joy and contentment in my relationships—but to no avail. I was perhaps looking in all the wrong places and shy of commitment.

It was then that I started dating Morgan, Chae's cousin. Morgan came into my life at a time when I was pretty desperate to make a relationship work. I was tired of my college sexy stud image. I wanted to be more than just a one-night stand. Everything about Morgan was exciting—from her long, curly red hair, sensual lips that curved into a perpetual pout, and her shapely legs—everything that is—except her conversation. I once told her how I grew up on a lonely farm, miles away from civilization.

"You mean they didn't ever have air conditioning or wall-to-wall carpeting?" she'd asked, disgusted. "How did you ever manage to survive? Talk about Neanderthal!" After that, I stopped sharing those memories from my past. Instead, I focused on the present. After all, wasn't that what mattered?

It was a chance remark from Morgan, while we were seated in

a small French bistro that ultimately changed the course of my life. "You know Taylor," she said grasping my arm, "you remind me of my cousin with all that boring talk."

"What boring talk?" I tried to ask jovially.

"Oh, you know. The trivia you keep throwing at me."

I sat stark still. Collecting trivia was one of my passions. I could never find a girlfriend who appreciated it. "You don't have to humor me, you know. If you don't like hearing it, you could always say so."

Morgan giggled; her tinkling, bell-like laughter rang throughout the room. "Oh, no. Really, I think it's kind of cute," she told me. "But it only gets to be too much when I go home. My cousin still lives there, and she unloads all that stuff on me, too. I mean, twice a day is more than any girl can bear." She rolled her eyes.

I remembered that Morgan had been brought up by an uncle who lived in the countryside, about an hour's drive from the city. In spite of myself, I was intrigued. "Your cousin? You've never mentioned a cousin before"

She smiled to herself as she spoke. "It must have slipped my mind. Besides, she's hardly anyone important. She likes the other boring things you do—like bird-watching and chess."

"Too bad I didn't meet her first! Maybe you should introduce us," I joked.

Morgan seemed startled for a moment. Had she taken me too literally? After a slight pause, she said, "Maybe I will. I'm sure you both would get along real fine. Too bad she doesn't have the other assets you'd be looking for!"

I didn't catch the odd smirk on Morgan's face, I was too distracted by the waiter who had brought us our food. He had slipped on the rug and a bowl of steaming bouillabaisse landed right in my lap.

She stiffened, momentarily abashed. Then, Morgan screamed out in both shock and pain.

Drenched and disgusted, I stood up. "Let's get out of here," I muttered.

The evening pretty much went downhill from there. Morgan hadn't liked the abrupt way in which we'd left. She also hated having the take-out food I'd bought for her afterward.

"I'm sorry but I couldn't eat with food all over me,"

I apologized when we were back in my apartment, but she looked sulky.

"The manager did apologize, you know," I said, wondering what would have happened if the soup had landed on her. You made too much of a fuss!"

I guess it was at that moment that I knew that Morgan and I weren't an item. She was ill tempered and had absolutely no sense of humor. I couldn't imagine what life would be like married to her!

Once again, an inexplicable loneliness engulfed me. My thoughts wandered back to what she had said to me at the restaurant. "So what does this cousin of yours do?" I asked, attempting a nonchalance I didn't quite feel.

A wicked gleam lit up Morgan's eyes. "She's a fashion designer," she said, slowly. "You know, why don't you try to contact her, Taylor? She'd be perfect for you!"

For a moment, I was completely taken aback. Was Morgan so bored with me that she was trying to dump me on her cousin? But her cousin did sound interesting. She had me truly hooked.

"Sure," I said. "I wouldn't mind meeting a fellow bird-watching buddy."

"Good! I'll write down her email address for you."

"Don't you have her phone number?"

"It's out of order," Morgan snapped.

"You never told me what your cousin's name was," I countered.

"Chae," Morgan replied, shrugging into her fur coat.

"Sounds beautiful, like a song," I mumbled.

It didn't escape me that Morgan was trying her best to stifle her laughter. What was she finding so funny? Perhaps Chae is such a knockout, Morgan thinks she is out of my league? I thought. As I kissed Morgan good night that evening, my thoughts were far away. Hope, like a fledgling bird, was beating against my breast. Perhaps, I was destined for love after all!

It wasn't until the next week that I mustered up the courage to write to Chae. Did she look anything like Morgan, I wondered idly. After all, they were blood relations. Perhaps Chae would be the combination of beauty and brains—my dream woman. My fingers trembled as I typed out my message, introducing myself and highlighting my hobbies.

She replied that very day. Hello Taylor, it's so wonderful to get to know you. I was amazed at how much we have in common! Morgan hasn't mentioned you before, but I suppose you've known each other a long time?

Too long, as far as I was concerned. The minute I read Chae's letter, I knew Morgan was only a distant memory. Chae had a way of making you feel good about yourself. The warmth of her personality shone through her words.

It filled me with so much joy, that her messages soon became the focal point of my day. I'd switch on the computer and settled into my swivel chair as I brushed my teeth, waiting expectantly as her mail downloaded. We exchanged trivia like never before, sharing exciting tidbits several times a day. Finally, I'd found someone who understood and appreciated my quirk! We would constantly vie with each other to flaunt the best facts and throw in a little humor for good measure.

Did you know that in Pennsylvania, the ministers are forbidden for performing marriages when either the bride or groom is drunk? Chae wrote. I think it's because they wanted them to realize exactly where their headache was coming from the day after!

That's a good one! I typed in reply. But let's see you top this! Did you know that nearly 50% of the world is sleep deprived?

After many such exchanges, I noticed that one of my trivia facts had bothered her: On planet Jupiter, you would weigh nearly three times what you would on earth! Maybe that's where all our undernourished beauty queens should go! I wrote.

I was puzzled when she didn't reply several days after that. I felt I had somehow offended her.

Then, her mail popped into my box again, and all was right with the world.

Does that mean you dislike thin woman? Chae wrote.

Not dislike exactly, but let's just say I do prefer hugging curves, and not getting injured by the bones, I wrote with a goofy grin.

After that, things suddenly got more personal. Chae asked me a host of questions about myself, and soon, my preferences and feelings were the highlight of every letter we exchanged. When I asked her to talk about herself, she was reserved. Not being one to pry, I didn't push her. I was willing to take whatever she had to offer and on her terms.

One morning, I threw all caution to the wind. I think I'm deeply in love with you, I wrote. You're one very amazing woman. I waited in anticipation for her reply. When it came, I was disappointed.

You can't possibly be in love with me, she said, the realist as always. We haven't even seen each other! You wouldn't know me from Eve!

Love doesn't begin with the eyes, I wrote back. I don't care about Eve, but I know deep in my heart that I care about you—very much. I want to marry you, to be a part of your life forever.

Morgan and I had gone on a few more dates, but they weren't very memorable. Perhaps, it was because I couldn't wait to get back home and see what Chae had written about my latest offering. The fact that I'd hit it off so well with her cousin, seemed to please Morgan.

"Oh you both should meet, Taylor. Imagine having exchanged all those mails without even having seen how she looks like!" she said with saccharine sweetness, one evening when I had thanked her for "introducing" us.

"Yes, well, I suppose we should—especially since we don't live all that far away." I said hesitantly. I wasn't very sure why I didn't jump at the chance of meeting Chae. I was uncharacteristically nervous. What if she hates me? I didn't want to lose something so precious to me, a relationship that I was just beginning to explore— so new, different, and fascinating. Even Chae seemed to share some misgivings about meeting in person. She had turned a deaf ear to my entreaties to send me her photograph. Ironically, it was Morgan who brought us together—only, as I learned later, with the sole intention of pushing us apart.

When Morgan first invited me to her big party Friday night, I was inclined not to go, at first. Classes were hectic, and I'd just finished a grueling round of exams. Sleep had eluded me for weeks, and I was dead tired. When I declined, Morgan persisted. Finally, one argument clinched it.

"You know it's the perfect chance to meet Chae, don't you?" Morgan said, a malicious gleam in her eyes. "After all, it is her birthday and I am throwing the party in her honor."

"Party for Chae?" I questioned.

"Oh, you mean you didn't know? We're celebrating at my uncle's ranch house. That's about ten miles from here. It's where Chae lives now. She moved back awhile ago."

"I . . . I'd be happy to make it," I stammered. I was embarrassed that my face had turned beet red.

Morgan appraised my change with a cool look. "I thought you'd see it my way," she said, quietly. "I really look forward to having you there, Taylor," she smiled.

"Tha . . . thanks." I stammered again, confused.

I spent the intervening days dreaming of the moment when I'd meet Chae in the flesh. Will it be love at first sight? Will I take her in my arms the moment our eyes met and press my lips to hers? After all, we'd gotten to know each other well before we'd known how the other even looked.

We couldn't be classified as strangers. Not by a long shot. Why, I knew things about Chae that even her family hadn't an inkling of. Things that were private and personal—like how much she was addicted to chocolate, or how she loved lace lingerie. I'd sent her letters telling her how excited I was to meet her, but oddly enough, her response was only lukewarm.

I thought she was just plain embarrassed because Morgan had insisted on throwing such a big party in her honor. I had almost revised my opinion of Morgan, then.

Friday dawned bright and early. The day before, I'd sent Chae three different birthday cards—a funny one, a sentimental one, and a card that was full of melody, set to the tune of a touching, sensitive love poem. I knew each of those cards would appeal to different aspects of Chae's personality. I also spent the entire day shopping. That evening, armed with a dozen crimson red roses and a box of Swiss chocolates, I drove to the address that Morgan had given me. I'll admit that chocolates and roses weren't the most original gifts in the world, but I knew that the solitaire diamond ring I had purchased that morning, would more than make up for it.

I'd planned to propose to Chae that night. I knew that, sometimes, the traditional way worked best. I had splurged recklessly on the ring, putting in a year's savings from my part-time job as a stock analyst as the down payment. But I didn't regret it for a minute. Chae deserved only the best, I thought. Little did I know that that night would shatter my illusions and tear my short-lived happiness to shreds!

It was a little past eight when I stepped into Chae's home. The colonial-style ranch house seemed inviting and spacious. There were extensive lawns, and wide, swaying oak trees. Morgan spotted me seconds after I pulled up in my red minivan.

"Taylor, good to see you!" She trailed her frosted pink nails across the front of my shirt as she leaned over and pecked my cheek.

I smiled distractedly. Where is Chae? Is she coming out to see me? Is she busy with the guests? My mind barely registered how enticing Morgan looked. She was wearing a hot pink miniskirt that showcased her miles of sleek, creamy legs. The skirt ended in a ruffle that clung gently to her thighs. Her lipstick and eye shadow were bright neon pink. Somehow, I was sure Chae would dress more subtly.

"So where's the birthday girl?" I asked brightly. All the while, my heart raced to a nervous, exciting beat.

"Oh, she's inside, waiting for you." Morgan grabbed my sleeve and led me into the house. The air was warm and smelled distinctly of hot scones and mouth-watering pastries.

"Chae would probably bake her own birthday cake if I let her," Morgan said as she laughed. "She insisted on making homemade scones for the guests, though. She really has a way with food, you know."

Again, there was that look of pure devilment in Morgan's eyes, but, as usual, I was too distracted to question it. It wasn't until later that I realized how much hidden implication there was tucked away behind Morgan's seemingly innocent remarks. I clutched my red roses and box of chocolates tightly to my chest, and followed Morgan into a crowded, spacious kitchen. There were nearly ten people seated around a worn wooden table in an informal dining area. They were all laughing and talking as if they were old friends. Music blared from a speaker overhead. My eyes scanned the crowd expectantly. They stopped on a petite girl with bleached blond hair, styled very much like Morgan's.

I glanced at Morgan, who was grinning from ear to ear. "Well, do you see your dream woman in here?" she asked, mocking me, her hands on her hips.

I walked over to the table and stood next to the pretty woman with blond hair. "Chae?" I asked, smiling hesitantly.

To my horror, there was no answering smile, nor any sign of recognition in her eyes. She merely looked curious. After pausing for a brief instant, the lady pointed to the space behind me. "Chae's over there by the oven," she said.

I whirled around, and came face to face with the woman whose vibrant personality had filled my days with joy for the past three months. My eyes widened with surprise.

Above the muted whispers and cacophony, Morgan's loud laughter pierced the air between us. I could feel my face growing red, could feel everyone around me staring, but I didn't care. I stood locked in place, rooted to the spot by deep shock and a drowning embarrassment. I had let the roses fall to the floor, but was still clutching the box of chocolates.

"Hello Taylor. It's so nice to meet you at last," Chae said, walking up to me with a smile. "You're just like I'd imagined."

There seemed to be a note of sadness in her voice, an almost wistful longing that I shrank from. To say Chae was as unlike the mental image I'd created of her, was the understatement of the century. It wasn't that Chae was plain or ugly. She had lovely blue eyes, and a charming smile. What I found so revolting was the fact that she was huge—so obese it was obscene! At one hundred eighty pounds, she took up all the space as she ambled along the corridors or stood by the doorway. Her baggy skirt hung over her huge frame like an extra large potato sack. She had thick black hair, but it was pushed into a sloppy ponytail that trailed halfway down her back. Her face was completely devoid of makeup, and she wore no jewelry—no feminine trinkets of any kind.

I was beginning to see what a cruel joke Morgan had played on me. After the initial shock, I collected my wits about me long enough to mumble happy birthday greetings, and I thrust the chocolates into her arms.

She winced at the abruptness of my greeting, and bent down to pick up the roses that lay scattered at her feet. "Why don't you two lovebirds talk in the den?" Morgan giggled, as she steered us both out of the room.

I glared angrily at her. The minute we stepped into the den and shut the door behind us, a babble of voices broke out from the kitchen. It seemed that Morgan was enjoying giving everyone a blow-by-blow detail of how I'd dumped her for her lard bucket of a cousin. The muted exclamations and the derisive laughter reverberated through the house.

The one overpowering feeling I carried away with me about the day we first met, was that of deep disgust. I was also feeling very sorry for myself. It was as though the woman I had dreamed of had died, and I was mourning her loss. To this moment, I still feel deeply ashamed at how I behaved that night. Why haven't I been able to appreciate Chae for herself, for what a beautiful human being she is on the inside? I thought. I admire her to no end before I even set eyes on her. So what exactly has changed? Why do I feel so cheated, so deceived?

To be honest, I didn't quite know, myself. I sighed and realized with a start that Chae had been observing my every move. None of the emotions that had played across my face now, had escaped her quick eyes. Embarrassed, I was determined to make up for it by acting as casual as I possibly could.

The den was a cozy room filled with comfortable leather easy chairs. "Won't you sit down Taylor," she said pointing to an overstuffed ottoman. I sank into the plush upholstery. My body was still tense and wary.

"Thank-you for the roses and the box of chocolates," she continued. Her gentle voice had a soft, almost lyrical quality to it. At least that was one thing that worked out the way I'd imagined. I shut my eyes for a brief second, willing myself to respond normally. The diamond ring I had purchased in a moment of reckless abandon was now burning a hole through my pocket. I swallowed nervously, and avoided meeting her eyes.

Chae cleared her throat. "You can look at me Taylor, I don't bite, you know." There was the hint of tears in her voice. I glanced up and looked away again, managing a weak laugh. "Of course, you don't."

"At least not me, anyway," I blurted out. The minute the words were out, I regretted them instantly. I could feel Chae squirm on the couch next to the ottoman, but mercifully, she let my dumb remark pass.

"You have quite a nose for trivia. Where do you pick up your facts?" she asked. On more neutral ground, I began to relax a little. "From the Internet, quiz books, health sites, encyclopedias—you name it!" I smiled for the first time that evening. "You're pretty good yourself," I remarked.

She shrugged. "I try," she said slowly. "But not too many people are interested; they think trivia is boring."

"It certainly isn't, at least not the way you present it," I said, warmly.

She gave me a watery smile.

Somehow, that suddenly irritated me.

89

She was cheerful and smiling while I was hurting so badly inside. And Morgan, her cousin, was laughing at me behind my back.

I could feel the anger coursing like slow poison through my system. How dare they play with my feelings like this? I wanted to hurt the fat woman seated next to me. I wanted to make her pay for my foolishness. "Do me a favor," I said through gritted teeth as Chae looked up expectantly. "Don't ever go to Jupiter—if you weighed three times more than you do now, then you'd just blow up!" My laugh was hollow and died in my insides when I saw raw pain register on her face.

She crumpled on the sofa as I fled from the room. I yanked open the front door, revved the engine of my car, and ran from the scene of my crime as fast as I could. Chae's sobs still echoed in my mind. I couldn't believe I had been that cruel, that insensitive. That evening was the worst disaster in my life, and I was determined to never repeat it. Who needed female company anyway? I was determined to live like a monk.

Two weeks after my resolve, I was dating Morgan again. It was exactly what Morgan had planned. One look at her cousin, and she knew I would be eating out of her hand. I'm mortified to admit that she was right! I couldn't appreciate her flashy beauty enough after that ordeal. I took Morgan out to the movies, restaurants, musicals, and on long drives in the country.

On most of these trips, I noticed that we would end up at her uncle's ranch house. I learned later that Morgan had always been jealous of Chae's popularity and intelligence. Though Chae was overweight, it didn't take me long to figure out how much people gravitated toward her, and how much they respected, loved and cherished her. Flaunting me before her cousin was Morgan's only way of taking revenge. She enjoyed it. That's why on our weekly outings, we'd end up quite close to the ranch and inevitably, she'd invite me home. I always declined on these instances.

Six weeks later, on one of our drives by the ranch, I caught sight of a lonely, forlorn figure in an oversized sweat suit, jogging in the distance. I looked confused for a second, but Morgan was quick to enlighten me.

"That's Chae," she said, gleefully. "She's taken to exercise. Jogs about five to six hours every day, and she eats only rabbit food."

Something about Chae bothered me. I couldn't get the image of her in the sweat suit out of my mind. The next morning, I made the trip alone. It was close to noon when I pulled up at the ranch. Sure enough, there she was in the same blue sweat suit. How long had she been exercising? I swallowed nervously. I wanted to approach her, tell her to rest a while, but something held me back. I was ashamed of the way I'd behaved the night of her birthday party, and I didn't know how my concern would be accepted. Who could blame her if she told me to butt right out of her life and mind my own business? Our e-mails had abruptly stopped. I hadn't had any contact with her at all since the fiasco in her home. In her eyes, I would be nothing but the cruel, unsupportive man who had not only bitterly rejected her, but had utterly humiliated her in the process.

Yet, for months afterward, I was drawn to the ranch of my own accord. Guilty conscience, perhaps? Somehow, I knew it was more than just that. I missed Chae, and yet, I was the one who had rudely ended our communication. For the fifth time that week, I sighed as I pulled the Chevrolet into a curb, near the ranch. Scrambling out, it took me a few seconds to adjust to the bright sunshine. Shading my eyes with my hands, I scanned the fields. In minutes, I caught sight of her again. There, she was in her blue sweat suit, jogging alone—a solitary figure silhouetted in the morning light.

Was it my imagination, or did she look different, somehow? I knew I had to speak to her. I promised myself I wouldn't hedge out of it this time. I exchanged my dress shoes for running gear and shrugged out of the jacket I had donned for my eleven o clock meeting with the corporate heads of a company that would be hiring me full-time next fall. The gravel crunched underfoot as I jogged in the direction in which I had just seen Chae emerge. I didn't want to startle her, so I called out to her as I ran.

"Chae!" I yelled, waving my arms wildly. "Wait!" For a second, she stood motionless, then slowly turned around. I could see the shock in her eyes as she caught a glimpse of me. Then, to my horror, she simply turned around, and continued jogging. I ran after her for a few minutes, before I stopped out of breath. This is ridiculous, I thought. Who would've thought she could run so fast? And I was supposed to be the fit one—all six feet of lean hard muscle and washboard abs. The sun was beating down my back and I was sweating bullets.

I turned tail and headed for the ranch. It was an hour before she finally showed up. She had probably waited for me to leave. I hid behind a few bushes and pounced on her as she passed the front door.

"Chae, you've got to listen to me!" I said.

She screamed and bolted, but I caught her hand in mine and forced her to turn around and face me. "Look, I treated you so badly the other night. I wanted to tell you how sorry I am," I said, quietly. "You didn't deserve to be insulted that way. I'm such an insensitive bore. Will you forgive me?"

Chae shook off my hand and settled into one of the white wicker chairs on the front porch. She sighed. "You don't have to apologize, Taylor. You were just being honest, I guess," she claimed. I settled down next to her, and we talked that day—really talked. "I've always been overweight," she confessed. "Ever since my parents' divorced, I think food became a sort of comfort. I always had a low self-esteem, and binging on food just helped me confirm that image of myself. It also helped me get through that traumatic phase in my life."

"It's over, now," I said, soothingly, holding her hand in mine.

"Yes, but old habits die hard," she said, a wry smile on her face. "I guess I should thank you, Taylor."

"For what? For being the biggest jerk in all fifty states?"

"No, for listening now, and for giving me enough incentive for wanting to change the way I look."

With the apology off my chest, for the first time, I marveled at the change I was seeing in Chae. She was swimming in the blue sweatpants now, and she looked only half the size that she'd had on the night of her birthday party. Her face was glowing with energy, and I could actually see how beautifully those blue eyes sparkled. "I'm eating healthier, now," she told me, proudly. "I've dropped about forty pounds in the past four months!"

"Forty pounds! Is that. . . that all right?" I asked awkwardly. "I mean, aren't you going too fast?"

"No," she said firmly. "When you left that night, I knew I had to get rid of all this flab. I couldn't do it soon enough."

"But forty pounds in four months. . . are you consulting a specialist?"

"I don't need to. Their diets never worked for me. I'm eating having soups and celery, and exercising for about four hours a day. For the first time in my life, I'm shedding pounds faster than I'm piling them on! It's amazing. I feel great!"

Her enthusiasm was infectious. I hugged her, and asked her out Saturday night.

She declined softly. "Not just yet," she said, puzzling me.

During the next few months, a whirlwind of activity had taken over my life. I was graduating, and had been to many on-campus interviews. It was a crucial period in terms of my career, and I had little time to socialize. I had broken up with Morgan a long time ago. She was the one who had finally called it quits. She had found a rich fiancé, and couldn't be bothered with me, anymore.

I hadn't minded. I was still exchanging trivia and emails with Chae. She kept me updated on her diet and fitness regime. I encouraged her all I could, though I hadn't seen her in months. Then, one night, out of the blue, she invited me to dinner.

Armed with another bouquet, I went to the ranch. It was to be a simple, home-cooked meal, and I was looking forward to seeing once her again.

The door was opened by a stunning beauty, dressed in a swirling green skirt with a plunging neckline that set off her perfectly toned body. After gaping for a few seconds, I gathered my wits about me enough to ask whether Chae was at home. The young woman laughed. "Don't tell me I'm as changed as all that!" she exclaimed. "You're enough to kill any girl's ego, Taylor." I could hardly believe my eyes. Was that really Chae? The transformation was astounding. She looked so slim, fit—absolutely gorgeous.

Once again, I was speechless as I gazed at her—this time with unbridled delight. I took her into my arms, and held her tight. "You did it!" I exclaimed.

I was very proud of her. For the first time, we kissed, and all other thoughts flew out of my head. I couldn't get over how incredibly beautiful she had become. After that night, we started seeing each other in earnest. I was eager to make amends for the hurt I had so thoughtlessly inflicted on Chae in the past. Our courtship was magical. On some nights, we hit the local discos and danced entwined in each other's arms until the wee hours of the morning. On others, Chae rustled up the most delicious home-cooked meals, and we would sit toasting marshmallows in a roaring fire, sharing our secrets, and enjoying quiet companionship. On one of these occasions, I'd inquired about her parents.

"Dad died after a massive heart attack, leaving me the ranch three years ago," she said. "I wanted to be a fashion designer, then, but I couldn't leave him here alone. So I moved back. It was my childhood home. I couldn't bear to sell it."

"And your mother?"

"I haven't seen my mother in years. She disappeared after the divorce. She just broke our hearts and walked out of our lives. Dad never really recovered. Things went downhill since then for him."

"I'm sorry," I said softly.

"That was a long time ago." She blinked away her tears as I massaged her shoulders. "Dad should've taken care of himself better. His whole family had a history of heart failure, but he just let the pressure get to him, anyway. There wasn't anything I could do."

I understood the demons that had chased her. I felt her pain and longed to erase those memories. I proposed that evening.

At first, she just stared at the ring and for a terrifying moment, my heart was in my throat. I thought she would refuse.

Instead, she burst into tears and kissed me wildly.

Three months later, we were married. My parents flew down for the wedding to meet Chae. Everyone was enamored of my beautiful, blushing bride. Chae looked gorgeous in her pure white wedding gown, decked out in lace and frill. Her azure eyes glowed with health and vitality.

As we exchanged vows, I knew life couldn't get better than this. I thanked the Lord for the very precious gift He had given me—the gift of love. Little did I know that Chae was already marching headlong into the dark abyss of death.

We were going to honeymoon in Paris. I had booked us on the first flight to Europe. We sped away to the airport after our ceremony. It was late night when we reached our hotel. Chae looked exhausted, but I thought it was because of all the excitement. I carried her in my arms over the threshold of the hotel room. I'll never get over the shock and despair that I experienced in the next few moments. It all happened so fast.

One minute, Chae was giggling about how hopelessly romantic I was, and the next minute; she was doubled over with pain. I set her down on the bed and was shocked to see how pale she looked. She was sweating profusely, and she couldn't move her left arm. Sheer panic rose to my throat as I frantically attempted to reach a doctor. Chae's whole body was wracked with convulsions and she was clutching her chest. In a few short minutes, the woman I loved breathed her last breath in my arms.

The medical verdict was a massive cardiac arrest. She had lost too much weight too soon, and it had put a great deal of pressure on her heart. In what was the darkest period of my life, I grieved the loss of a woman who was so much a part of me. Even today, I believe that Chae and I are inseparable in death as we were for that brief blissful period in life. She still lives on inside me. I also know that I can never forgive myself for what happened. If it hadn't been for my initial rejection of her, Chae would never have taken it into her head to exercise herself to the grave!

Carrying that burden around with me every day makes my loneliness more intense, until grief cuts me anew. How I long to join my Chae—to find release from this cage of flesh that traps me! I can only pray for deliverance. Even if the good Lord forgives me, I hope that one day, I will be able to forgive myself for so unintentionally wronging the only woman I truly loved. Until then, I shall cherish the sweet memories of Chae, and bask in the warmth of her personality, dreaming of the moment when we shall meet again.

THE END

PREGNANT BY
THE WRONG BROTHER

The tiny bridal shop was a flurry of activity as bridesmaids tried on dresses. Kendra, the bride, was my husband's twin sister. It was her idea that each attendant wear a different color of the same style dress. I appraised my reflection in the mirror. Okay, I admit it, I was preening. But I felt so good, on top of the world.

Things were finally looking up for Steve and I after a very rocky two years. I was pregnant. Elated, I told everyone. My happiness reflected itself in the mirror. The peach hue of the bridesmaid dress suited my hair color and complexion. I glowed. Tugging on the bodice of the dress, I was pleased to note that for once I filled out my clothes. My bust was womanly with the first signs of my pregnancy. In the past I'd always been embarrassed by my small chest.

Stepping back, I looked at my waistline to see if the pregnancy was in evidence at three months. In the mirror my eyes met those of Katie, Kendra's maid of honor. There was pure venom in her eyes. I was shocked. We hardly knew each other. She had gone to school with Kendra and my husband. What could I have done to make her display such open hostility?

Gathering the full skirt of my dress, I turned and left the dressing room, nearly colliding with someone. A pair of strong arms held me. I looked up.

"Josh! You're not supposed to be here," I admonished my brother-in-law. Steve's older brother was as tall and good looking as the entire Anderson family, but not nearly as charismatic as my Steve. Yet his eyes held a compassion that Steve's didn't.

"I think that's just the groom," he chided. "I'm here to drive the bridesmaids to the luncheon." He seemed to suddenly notice his hands still on my arms and removed them quickly. Looking me up and down he said, "You're radiant, Phoebe! Pregnancy agrees with you. How are you feeling?"

"Really great," I assured him.

"Steve's treating you right?" he questioned.

"Of course! He's so excited about this baby."

"If you need anything—"

"Josh, don't," I interrupted. "He's really changed."

He gave me a quick hug and said, "Okay, okay. I'm sorry."

I didn't like to think about the last few years. I met Steve at a convention in Baltimore. It was love at first sight. Who wouldn't have fallen for him? He was the man of my dreams, of every girl's dreams. That he was pursuing me, plain old Phoebe Chandler, was unthinkable. Steve had a charm that made you think you're the only girl in the world. With his lethal looks, those killer eyes, and that thick hair, I was entranced.

Our long-distance courtship lasted about six weeks. I commuted from Harrisburg to Baltimore every weekend. Then Steve insisted we shouldn't wait any longer. We were married in his parents' home.

I was an only child. My parents were much older. They died several years ago. Steve's parents really welcomed me into the family. They were relieved to see Steve settling down. He and his twin sister, Kendra, had a notoriously wild youth. Josh, on the other hand, was—and still is—more reserved.

The first year of marriage was too good to be true. Steve was thoughtful and doting. A wonderful lover, he initiated me into the pleasures of sexual passion. Totally enamored, I was devoted to pleasing him. I didn't notice, didn't want to see the signs, that something was amiss. It was Josh who came to me and told me the truth while Steve was gone on a business trip.

"Phoebe, there's something I have to talk to you about."

"Is Steve all right?" I remember asking, sensing impending doom.

"No, he's fine. Phoebe, there's been talk." He couldn't look me in the eyes.

"Josh, what is it?" I became frantic.

"Steve's having an affair," he blurted out.

"What? That's a lie!" I screamed at him. I began to cry, softly at first, and then I couldn't stop. In my heart I knew it to be true. All the signs were there. Late nights, money unexplainably missing from our checking account, mysterious phone calls. Only an idiot wouldn't have figured it out. But I didn't want to know.

I cried and cried. Josh held me. He tried to convince me to leave Steve, but I couldn't. I was so in love with my husband. There had to be a way to fix things. I'd be a better wife, I resolved. We'd go to counseling.

I decided to confront him when he got home. He walked in the door and kissed me. "Oh, Phoebe," he told me. "I've missed you so much."

Those drugging kisses of his. We were making love before I could think about anything else. I never did talk to him about Josh's accusations. Steve was so loving and attentive. How could I? Besides, if he was having an affair, it was over now. My old Steve was back, that's all that mattered. I blamed myself. How could I expect to keep a man like Steve with my plain looks?

I wasn't surprised when, a few months later, the signs started appearing again. They were bolder that time. We never made love anymore. He was too tired. I was so trusting, so naive. I realized I'd have to find out what was going on if I wanted to save my marriage. I called Josh and told him of my suspicions.

"Phoebe, I'll do what I can."

"Please! Just talk to him."

"What my brother needs is a little shock to the system. Phoebe, you're always there for him, the devoted wife. He has no worries. Shake him up a little."

That night I thought about what Josh said. He was right. I'd become Steve's safe haven. Good little Phoebe, always there. I packed my bags and wrote Steve a short note.

I checked into a motel. I didn't know what I was going to do, but I needed time to think. One thing for sure, I wasn't emotionally strong enough to see Steve. If he even touched me I'd be lost. He knew the power he had over me. I waited three days before I called him.

"Phoebe, where are you? What's going on?" His voice sounded anxious.

"Steve, I want a separation. I'm not sure if I want to be married to you anymore."

"That's crazy! Where are you? We need to talk, Phoebe."

"No."

"You can't just make a decision like that without talking to me. Please."

"Steve, you made the decision when you cheated on me."

"I'm sorry. It didn't even mean anything."

There was silence on the line. At least he didn't try to lie to me. I thank God for that. What I didn't realize was that Josh had visited him, raking him over the coals about his behavior. For the time being, Steve was repentant.

"How long, Phoebe? When can I see you?" he asked quietly.

I closed my eyes, feeling warm tears slipping down my cheeks. Holding my hand over the receiver, I took a deep breath and cleared my throat. "I don't know," I told him, my voice wobbly.

"I love you, Phoebe."

I hung up the phone, unable to stop the tears. Wiping my eyes with my hands, I whispered, "I love you, too."

Over the next few months, I fell into a pit of depression. My life had revolved around Steve for so long that I didn't know what to do without him. Josh helped me find a small apartment with a monthly lease. I was certain I'd soon be going home to my husband. Still, one month turned into two, and I didn't hear anything from Steve. I came home to an empty apartment each night after work, imagining him out on the town with beautiful women. Most nights I cried myself to sleep, wallowing in self-pity.

That was how Josh found me one weekend. I answered the door on a Saturday afternoon, still in my robe. I didn't have the energy to shower or even comb my hair.

"Phoebe, are you sick? Why didn't you call me?" He brushed past me into the apartment, taking charge. "Come on, sit down."

"No, Josh. I'm not sick," I told him, flopping into a chair like a rag doll.

"This is ridiculous! You're letting my brother do this to you?" he accused angrily.

I looked up, surprised. He rarely said unkind things. Instead, he was always tactful and diplomatic.

"Go take a shower," he ordered. "We're getting out of this place."

He took me downtown to the community college and picked up a catalogue. Refusing to tell me where we were going, he headed the car out of town. We ended up at a neighborhood park. Parking in the shade, he reached over to the backseat, collecting the containers of food he picked up at the last town we'd passed.

"C'mon," he said cheerfully, walking toward the beach. His enthusiasm was contagious. I ran to catch up with him.

Sitting down at a picnic table, I watched him set out our meal. What a good man he was. He looked a lot like Steve with a cocky and mischievous grin, his hair tousled from the breeze off the lake. For a moment I let myself wonder what would've happened if I'd met him before I met Steve.

"Phoebe?" He peered down at me quizzically.

"What? Did you say something?"

He laughed. "Yeah, let's eat." He sat down beside me and dug into his food.

It was an idyllic afternoon. I felt more alive than I had in weeks. After we ate, Josh brought out the college information he had picked up.

"Think about it at least," he encouraged. "Taking a night class might be just what you need."

"I'm not going to forget Steve," I told him firmly.

His voice became tense and irritated. "That's not what I'm telling you. You just need to feel good about yourself again."

"Okay, Josh. I'll think about it."

In the end, I knew he was right. I needed to start building up my confidence, instead of hiding in the apartment. I enrolled in a literature class. I began to look forward to the class, which met two nights a week. Usually, some of us went out for coffee afterward. We had lively discussions about books and different authors. Sometimes I'd see a person who resembled Steve and freeze, thinking it was him. My hopes would sink when I realized it wasn't him. Pretty soon, I stopped hoping. Which is why one night in late September, I was taken totally by surprise.

I parked my car on the street next to my building after class. Right after locking the car door, I heard my name called. It was dark and chilly; the wind picked up piles of leaves and tossed them into the air. Surely I was mistaken. As I moved toward my building, a shiver of goose bumps went up my arms. I hurried up the steps.

"Phoebe."

I turned my head. Steve stood in the shadows. He looked so good. His hair was windblown and his hands were in the pockets of his leather jacket. I bit my lip to stop myself from eagerly crying out to him. As I turned away from him, he called me again.

"Phoebe, please."

It was my undoing. I turned back. He ran to me and wrapped his arms around me, though I quickly stepped out of his embrace. It felt too good. I kept my distance as I invited him in to talk.

"How did you know where I live?" I asked while I filled his mug with coffee. I couldn't help but notice how right he looked on my couch.

"I followed you home from work," he admitted. "I tried to get your number, but my family wouldn't give it to me. They all read me the riot act. Josh threatened to beat me to a pulp if I came anywhere near you."

"Josh?"

"My family thinks a lot of you. I've begun to realize they're right. I treated you miserably. I've been such a kid. I wanted it all. A wife at home and the freedoms of a single guy." He looked in my eyes and continued, "It wasn't worth losing you, Phoebe. Can you ever forgive me?"

"Yes, Steve, I can forgive you," I told him. He reached for me. I moved away. I wouldn't be caught in his snare again. "But we can't go back to the way we were. If you want to start over, maybe we can try on my terms."

I made him court me. We dated and got to know each other all over again. I refused any intimacies. I was amazed that he agreed. He'd changed, but what I realized was that I'd changed, too. I was no longer the shy, insecure girl he married. I carried a new confidence and I stopped idolizing Steve.

I thought Josh would be pleased about the change in his brother, instead, he was furious. He came over about a month after Steve and I had started to date again.

"You're going to move back in with him?" He stood and watched me pack up boxes, disbelief on his face.

"He's my husband. Besides, Steve's changed. He's grown up. I think we can make it this time."

"Phoebe, you're so good. I can't watch him use you and throw you away."

I walked over to him, held his hands in mine, and looked into his eyes. He seemed so anguished.

"Josh, I'm going to make it work this time. Be happy for me."

"I can't, Phoebe, I'm sorry." He turned and walked out of the apartment.

Steve's parents were thrilled at our reconciliation. And three months later they were even happier to find out they'd be grandparents. We hardly saw Josh. He was cordial at family gatherings, but he politely turned down our invitations to dinner.

When my sister-in-law, Kendra, became engaged to one of Steve's old buddies, I invited the entire family over to celebrate. Josh again had other commitments. I questioned Kendra privately in the kitchen.

"Why is Josh avoiding us?"

"Phoebe, don't you know Josh's in love with you?"

I nearly dropped the dish I held. Shock didn't even describe my surprise. "Kendra, why didn't he say something?" I felt horrible. All the times I'd called him and asked for his support and advice. How cruel I'd been.

"I'm not sure he even realized it himself until you and Steve decided to get back together."

"Does Steve know?" I asked.

"Oh, yes. Steve was at my parents' house when Josh confronted him about your reconciliation. Josh threatened to break his arm if he hurt you again. They yelled at each other. Steve accused him of being in love with his wife. Josh grabbed him and held him against the wall. I've never seen Josh so livid. Suddenly, he just took his hands off Steve and stormed out of the house."

"This is awful. How can I face your parents?"

"This is hardly your fault, Phoebe. Josh will be fine. You don't need to get upset. You have a baby to think of." She patted my arm.

We went back into the living room together. Kendra walked over to her fiancé, Wesley, and whispered in his ear. Then she called out to Steve and I.

"Wesley and I want to officially ask you two to be in the wedding party. Will you be one of my bridesmaids, Phoebe? Of course, Wesley wants Steve to be his best man." She gave us an expectant smile.

We both were delighted to share Kendra and Wesley's happiness. Kendra gave me the details of the dress fittings and the bridesmaid luncheon to follow. They were scheduled for just a few short weeks away. Kendra told me how pleased she was that her best friend, Katie, had just moved back to town and was to be her maid of honor.

Katie had been a close friend to the twins during their high school and college years. She'd just gone through a messy divorce and was in low spirits. Steve and Kendra were anxious for me to meet her, as they were certain we'd like each other.

We didn't. It was obvious from the introductions at the bridal shop that this woman wasn't interested in getting to know me. She was standoffish and cold. It was almost as though she didn't like the fact that Steve and I were happy and going to have a baby. Perhaps her bad divorce made her envious of others' happiness. But the look of hatred I saw in the mirror concerned me.

I questioned Steve about her that night at dinner. He blew me off.

"Phoebe, you imagined it. Why would Katie hate you? She doesn't even know you."

"Maybe she's jealous of our happiness?" I asked him. "Didn't you say she's gone through a difficult divorce?"

"She'd never be jealous. She's one of my oldest friends. That's ridiculous. I don't want to talk about it anymore."

He left the room. This was all very peculiar. I knew I wasn't imagining things. But there wasn't anyone I could ask. I couldn't get Josh involved in my problems. The wedding was only four weeks away. Hopefully I wouldn't have to see Katie very much.

At the rehearsal dinner I sat next to Caroline, another bridesmaid. Steve sat on my right, with Katie next to him. Katie monopolized him with conversation most of the meal. Steve, Kendra, and Katie recounted stories of their wild college days. I tried to be patient. After all, this was Kendra's night. When the band started to play, Katie grabbed Steve's hand and pulled him to his feet. He looked at me.

I shrugged and turned away, but not before I saw Katie's triumphant grin. As they danced, Caroline leaned over to me and whispered, "If that were my man, I wouldn't let that she-devil anywhere near him."

"They're old friends," I explained. And yet I wondered. If Katie wanted Steve, why hadn't she gone after him years before? Why pursue him now?

Lost in my thoughts, I was startled by a strong hand on my shoulder. I looked up. It was Josh.

"Dance, Phoebe?"

"That's sweet of you, Josh. But no." I didn't want to be accused of encouraging my brother-in-law's attention.

He winked and squeezed my shoulder gently before he left.

Caroline leaned over again and sighed, her gaze following Josh. "I'd leap tall buildings for that man." She giggled and smiled at me.

I smiled back and agreed. Josh would always be someone special.

The wedding was the next afternoon. Everything went smoothly. Kendra was such a lovely bride. I avoided Katie and kept Steve close to my side. We left the wedding banquet a little early. I claimed fatigue and made certain my devoted husband drove us home. Well, I was tired.

Kendra and Wesley left for a prolonged honeymoon. I admit I did envy them. As my pregnancy progressed to the second trimester, I had more bad days than good days. My hormones were in upheaval. Steve seemed unable to handle my mood swings and worked longer hours.

My old feelings of inadequacy returned as I blossomed larger and larger. I became more and more irritable and suspicious of Steve. At the start of my seventh month I quit work on my obstetrician's advice. I had mild pre-eclampsia and he advised me to take it easy.

With more time on my hands, I became more and more paranoid that Steve was cheating on me. I made checks to his office. I searched through his pants pockets and his briefcase while he was in the shower. Fortunately there was nothing to indicate he was guilty. I felt relieved and tried to make it up to him by cooking special gourmet meals or buying him little gifts.

Nearly a month passed. Wesley and Kendra would be home any day from their trip. I called my mother-in-law and asked her for the spare key to Kendra's apartment. She thought it was sweet of me to offer to dust the place for the newlyweds. With a warning for me to take it easy and go slow, she dropped off the key.

Kendra lived in a complex downtown. It wasn't far from Steve's office. I rarely got down there lately, so I decided to stop by the office and surprise Steve. I missed him by minutes. He had already left for lunch. His secretary offered to page him. I told her it wasn't necessary. I left a note on his desk, telling him how much I loved him and headed for Kendra's place.

I'd forgotten about the flight of stairs outside her building. I felt like an old woman as I slowly climbed them. When I inserted the key in her door, I thought I heard noises inside. I decided it must be a television from another apartment. My mother-in-law would've known if the newlyweds had arrived home early. The place was dusty. I turned on some lights and pulled open the curtains. Starting down the hallway to do the same in the other rooms, I heard noises again. Maybe a radio was left on?

I pulled open the bedroom door.

"Oh my God!" It was Steve's voice.

I looked up at the sight of my husband and Katie in my sister-in-law's bed. Believe it or not, I started laughing. I couldn't stop. I turned and ran out of the apartment. The tears fell uncontrollably. I couldn't see where I was going as I descended the steps. Suddenly, I was falling. That's all I could remember.

Someone was holding my hand. I opened my eyes and looked around. I was in the hospital. Josh anxiously peered down at me, his hand clutching mine. His eyes were moist and red.

"The baby?" I whispered.

"It's a girl, Phoebe. She's premature and they have her in an incubator, but she's strong. She'll make it. She's just like her mother." He squeezed my hand, a tear sliding down his face.

"When can I see her?"

"Soon. You've lost a lot of blood. They need to transfuse you." He paused. "Steve's outside."

"I don't want to see him. Never again, Josh." I could feel myself getting more and more agitated, just remembering what happened earlier.

"It's okay, Phoebe," he soothed, brushing my hair back from my face.

The nurse entered the room. She asked Josh to step outside for a few minutes.

"I'll be back in a little while," he promised, squeezing my hand.

And he was. Josh was at my bedside every minute they allowed him to be. Two days later I was ready for discharge, though my little baby would remain in the neonatal unit. Josh waited while I packed my belongings for the trip home. I was going to stay with a friend from work for a few days until I decided what to do next.

I closed my suitcase and turned to face Josh. "I'm so sorry," I told him. "Can you ever forgive me?"

"Forgive you? For what?"

"Josh, you've given me so much. I hurt you by not even noticing your love."

"You were committed to your marriage. I had no right to love you."

"I've been so foolish. Steve can't change. I see that now." I turned my head, willing myself not to cry. The time for tears was over. I was a mother now; I needed to face my future and leave my past.

"Phoebe, I was foolish, too. I never wanted to pressure or confuse you. I didn't think I had the right to fight for your love. But never again, for me, either. I'm not leaving you or the baby."

He lifted my hand to his mouth and softly pressed his lips against my fingers, his eyes locking with mine.

I can only pity Steve. He ended up marrying Katie, but it didn't last long. Nor did any of his subsequent marriages.

It was touch and go with my little daughter, but she's perfectly fine. And she has two other sisters now.

I'm so lucky. I have it all. Three beautiful daughters and a completely devoted, wonderful husband. I'm more in love with him now than the day we married. I know how fortunate I am that Josh finally fought for our love. And I'm grateful I finally opened my eyes to see what was right in front of me all along.

THE END

A NEW BRIDE ASKS...
Did I do the wrong thing?

It was my own fault, I guess. Maybe worrying constantly about what I'd do if my husband were unfaithful to me was hurting my marriage and me. But I was a new bride and should have been thinking only blissful thoughts.

Actually, I never really believed John would ever look at another women. Our love was too intense and too perfect. Although John was a doctor and was exposed to flirtatious patients, nurses, and other hospital staff, I never felt jealous. Well, not until Desiree came to spend the day with us.

Desiree. That name sounded like the kind of woman who wanted to desire someone else's husband—mine!

Desiree Chapel had come within a hair of being Mrs. John Bowman. They were high school and college sweethearts and were practically engaged.

I had recently moved to the area, and I had met Desiree in church. She had introduced me to John. It's funny, but I think John and I felt the same magnetic pull the moment we met.

Three weeks later, John and I were married. Our marriage shocked the whole town. After all, everyone expected John to marry Desiree. It didn't matter much to us, though. We were wildly in love and only wanted to be together.

I don't think John and I had been married more than a month before she stopped by to see us.

"I hope we can all be friends," she said. She smiled as though she were truly happy.

Then she sat down and hung out with us awhile. We talked about the town and John's job at the hospital. Everything seemed quite pleasant.

Later I told him, "I thought it was nice of her to come." I was ashamed of myself for not liking her.

"After all, darling," I said, "if someone snatched you out from under my nose, I don't think I'd be very pleasant about it. I'd probably tear her hair out."

John just smiled and took me in his arms and kissed me. "I love you," he said. And those were exactly the words I wanted to hear.

Later, though, John would say something every once in a while about having seen Desiree downtown, or at the hospital, where she had enrolled in the nursing program. And he'd always mention that it seemed a shame that she couldn't find the right man.

That's when the green-eyed monster began to wrap his tentacles around me. It's easy to say jealousy is a stupid trap into which only the ignorant and the fearful fall. But when it happens to you, jealousy is a terrifying emotion that has no beginning.

For me, it started when John kept talking about running into Desiree. I'm certain the way John and I met had something to do with it, too. John had been her man. Each time he spoke about Desiree, I wondered if he was thinking about her. I wondered if the casual way he mentioned her name was only a cover for the relationship they were developing again.

I was beginning to feel better when John spoke the words that changed everything. "Why don't you ask Desiree over? She needs to get out the house."

I was so shocked I responded sarcastically. "Why doesn't she come over on Saturday and spend the whole day with us? We certainly don't need to be selfish and spend the day together."

I didn't think I could have been more stunned until John opened his mouth. "That's a great idea! I'll call her and ask her to come on Saturday. We'll all have fun." Then he kissed me on my forehead and headed back to the bedroom to call Desiree.

I couldn't help thinking he had to be kidding. Did he think I was going to enjoy playing host to his ex-girlfriend? Did he think that I was going to welcome her into my home?

Well, Desiree seemed happy to come over. I wasn't exactly, Mrs. Hospitality, but I didn't throw her out. However, John and she never seemed to notice. They laughed and talked as though they were the best of friends.

Eventually, they started talking about hospital gossip. And I felt even more left out. I didn't work there and didn't know the people who did. The two of them were in their own little world and were happy that I was not a part of it.

After lunch, John suggested that we all go for a walk on the beach.

"Oh, I couldn't possibly," I said, thinking of the dishes. "But you two go," I added, automatically. The second I'd said it, I could have bitten off my tongue. But it was too late.

"All right," John said. "We'll only be gone for an hour or so." And in a few short minutes, with no further coaxing of me to go along, they left.

I can't describe the turmoil that rose inside me after they left the house. My hands shook as I washed the dishes. Why didn't John ask to wait until I was finished? Of course, he wouldn't wait. Then he could be alone—with her! And I had pushed the two of them together. I was really stupid!

I hurried with the dishes, so I could join them. They had asked me to join them. So what if I surprised them? They shouldn't mind—especially since they were such good friends.And John wanted the three of us to be friends.

The beach had been swept clean by wind and the waves. It wasn't a great beach day; it had been cool earlier. I only saw a pair of footprints, so I assumed they were John's and Desiree's. I followed the footprints.

I had almost reached them when I saw Desiree and John in each other's arms. That's when I knew it was over. My marriage had ended before I had a chance to make it good. Desiree had been the woman he had always wanted. I had just been a temporary fling.

I tried to stop the tears that slid down my cheeks, but I couldn't. John still loved Desiree. I couldn't bear to hear those words from his lips. But I had to try to be an adult about it. Soon, they would return to what had been John and my love nest. I would have to pretend as though I hadn't seen them, even though my heart was breaking.

I started to run wildly back to the cottage. I was trying to outrun my despair, but I knew that I couldn't. I opened the door and ran into the living room. Then I eased my tired body onto the living room couch. I tried to stop the tears, but I couldn't. My body felt as though it was convulsing as sobs left it.

Finally, they returned. By then, I had washed my face so it didn't look as read as it had looked. I tried to sound calm, but it was difficult. I refuse to cry in his presence. He doesn't deserve that much satisfaction!

"You should have come. We had a great walk," John said as he smiled. "It's such a beautiful day."

Yes, a beautiful day to break my heart, I thought.

"That was until that nasty bug came along," Desiree said.

"I didn't think I'd ever be able to get it out of your eye," John said.

"Some doctor." Desiree laughed. "It took him ten minutes, standing there in the sand, to get a beach fly out of my eye!"

"A beach fly?" I echoed as my mind was dazzled by the impact of what they were telling me. "A beach fly. How wonderful!"

They both stared at me as though they thought I'd gone crazy. But I didn't care. John didn't want Desiree—he wanted me.

"I love you," John said. "You're a little crazy, but I adore you," he said. Then he kissed me soundly.

As I turned around Desiree looked a little embarrassed.

"I told you I didn't think it was a good idea to visit so soon, John," she said. "Men are so silly," she said as she addressed me. "They don't understand that a woman in love wants nothing more than to be with the man she wants."

Then John walked toward the kitchen and begun mumbling something about women ganging up on him.

Desiree turned to me and said, "I hope you and I can be friends. John is one of the best friends I've ever had. I think we mistook our friendship for something more. I'm glad that he found you; someone he can truly love. I never had the heart to end our relationship. But I didn't have to because he found you," she said.

"I'm glad we found each other," I said. "And I hope that we can be friends, too."

"Please don't tell John about what I said. I don't want to hurt him. We just never had that passion that it's obvious the two of you have."

"Your secret is safe with me," I said. "And I think we are going to be good friends."

And that was the beginning of our friendship and my marriage. I didn't feel as though Desiree was going to take away my husband. And I realized that he truly loved me; I just wasn't a quick fling. And I wouldn't have realized that if Desiree hadn't been honest with me. How could I not be a friend to her?

I was finally a new bride who could look forward to having a long, happy marriage.

THE END

ALL'S FAIR IN LOVE…
A jealous coworker threatened to steal him away, but I won't let her!

As I looked at my wedding gown, I couldn't believe I was marrying an on-the-rise corporate executive. The dress was beautiful, and I looked good in it, but I was still surprised that he wanted me.

My best friend, Nadine, had already found her Prince Charming—he was an upcoming attorney, but I was still hoping to find someone to love. But the right man never seemed to appear. So, when a man at a café that Nadine and I went to often began staring at me, I didn't think anything about it.

Nadine and I walked into a café, and sat down waiting for the waitress to come over and take our orders.

"It's hot today," Nadine replied. "I need to get home and take a quick shower."

"I know the feeling," I replied, fanning myself. "It's crowded in here, today. I mingled by the place constantly, not seeing such a crowd, but everyday brings differences to our being, don't it?"

"Whatever," Nadine replied. "I miss my hubby."

"He's a man on the move, and you should be so proud of him."

"And I am. There's a firm in California that's interested in him, but that would mean taking the Bar in California. I don't know if he's up for that, and I don't want to move to the left coast," she said, softly. "I've lived here all my life, and I don't want to leave. But I do love him so much."

"And that is the most important thing—the love you share for each other, Nadine. If I had a husband like yours, I'd go wherever he wanted."

"That's easier said than done. You're not in the situation, so you're on the outside looking in. Imagine being in my shoes, then you'd change your tune."

I stared at the waitress as she smiled, took our orders for beverages, and then left a basket of bread and some butter on the side. Instantly, I reached for bread and butter. As I began buttering the roll, Nadine followed my lead.

"I guess you're right. I'm just someone looking in who has never been in love, so how could I possibly imagine?" I replied, dimly.

I took a bite of my roll as I stared at the crowded restaurant. When my eyes hit the back of the room, I noticed a very handsome man eyeing me. I couldn't believe it. I turned left and right, thinking that he couldn't have been checking me out.

He gave me the most brilliant smile. I turned away again, and he was still watching me, but I had to be absolutely sure.

"Nadine, look at that table in the back. Tell me what you see."

Nadine followed my instructions as she gazed in the direction I had pointed toward.

"I see a very appealing man staring at my best friend. Why don't you go over there, and put him out of his misery? I told you often that women aren't sitting around waiting for men to make the first move. It's the century for women coming out of their shells, and going after what they want. I walked up to Jack, remember?"

I nodded my head as I took a sip of my drink.

"I think not. I'm not in the mood for rejection, and he's probably married with three children."

"Why would he reject you? You look good, and the man is staring at you."

I decided to change the subject, so I started talking about work. Thirty minutes later, Nadine and I were laughing over chitchat about our work, school, and her husband. Then, I looked up and saw the man walking toward the table.

"Hello, ladies," he said, in a deep voice. "I couldn't help but admire two beautiful looking women, so I had to come over and see if the one I was checking out was free. My name is Terrence."

He stared at me, and I was flabbergasted. Words failed me.

"I'm Nadine, and this is Jasmine," Nadine stated. "Please join us, but excuse me because I have to run to the ladies' room."

I was so nervous when she hurried off, that I was speechless. I reached for my glass instead, and took a long swallow of my diet soda to play it off.

"Hello, Jasmine. Your name is as pretty as you are. I was wondering if I could have your telephone number or your e-mail address. I would like to get to know you," he stated, plainly.

I was shocked into silence. I did have e-mail, but was this guy really interested, or was it another game? I was so tired of "playas."

I liked his attitude. He didn't try to give me a line. He just came straight out and said he was interested. I didn't believe him, though. I was trying to figure out what his game was.

"Did I say something wrong? I certainly didn't mean to upset or offend you in any way."

"Uh . . . no. I was just thinking for a minute."

"I hope that you were thinking which thing you were going to give me: your telephone number or your e-mail address. I'd be happy with either or both, whichever one you're more comfortable giving me."

"I . . . I just don't know."

"What do you usually do when a man ask for your number? I'm sure this isn't the first time," he said, softly.

I didn't want to tell him the truth: That I rarely had a man to ask for my phone number. I just wasn't the kind that was attractive to men.

"Well, I usually don't give, either. I'd rather get the guy's uh . . . uh, I mean yours."

I tried to sound as normal as possible. I didn't want him to know that he made me nervous.

"Okay, so I'll give you my e-mail address and business card with my telephone number. And please feel free to get in touch with me at any time. Here are two cards in case you lose one. I'd stay longer, but on my way to a business meeting. I'm really looking forward to hearing from you. You can call or e-mail me late tonight if you like. I'm going to be up a while. Please say good-bye to your friend, also."

"I will," I said.

"And I really look forward to hearing from you."

Then, he arose and walked away.

"I saw the entire thing," Nadine stated, as she resumed her seat. "I hope you e-mail tonight. Don't keep that man waiting."

I came back to reality as I stared at her.

"He's probably just interested in sex, and nothing more or less. Frankly, I just don't have the time to play whatever game it is that he wants to play."

"This is your chance to meet a very respectable man, who is interested in you because you're a very attractive and beautiful woman. Go for it. What do you have to lose?"

Nadine shook her head.

"You're going to e-mail him tonight because I have a good feeling. Let's hurry up, and eat, and then get back to your place, so we can turn on your computer and get this romance booming. I do know what I'm doing, so just trust me."

Nadine was just as excited as I was. I e-mailed him that night, and he sent me one in return. And that was the beginning.

Two months later, Terrence and I was a couple. He was the perfect man in my eyes. Our first date was to dinner in an intimate bistro. They had jazz on Thursday night. Although I never though that I enjoyed jazz, I enjoyed the music and the company.

Our next date was to a small art gallery. I had mentioned in passing that I liked art, and I hoped to learn a little more about it.

Well, he took that thought and made it a reality.

The following week, we went to a movie. It was an action-thriller. He said that was his favorite kind of movie. I didn't respond at all. Afterward, we went to a little café to eat.

"I wasn't sure if you enjoyed action movies, but they're among my favorite kind. I just wanted you to get an idea about the kinds of things I like. I know we're not always going to have the same taste, but I just want you to see what I like.

"Well, I'm glad you don't like foreign films with subtitles. They always bore me."

"Why would you think that would be the kind of move I would enjoy?" he inquired.

"Well, you're so smart. I figured the intellectual types go for those kinds of movies."

Then, he laughed loudly. He was still laughing when the waiter came to take our order. He apologized and said that he hated foreign films and had never considered himself an intellectual.

"I'm the kind of man that likes to do a variety of things, but watching foreign films has never been one of them. A perfect evening would be spending the evening with you anywhere doing anything. I just love to be in your company. You light up any room, any time."

I blushed at his words. Again, I could barely think much less speak.

"You don't have to blush when you know it's true. Jasmine, you are truly a beautiful woman. I feel honored every chance I get to spend time with you."

What more could a woman want to hear?

I was beginning to feel good about myself, and I realized that Terrence really did care for me because he showed it in so many little ways. He'd send me cards because he thought that I'd like them. Or he'd send unusual flower arrangements. He said roses were too plain for me, and I deserved something with a little more imagination.

Terrence was a man who knew how to romance a woman. We'd relax at his condo and he'd tell me about the latest deal he was working on. Or he'd grill a steak, make a salad, and bring home a delicious desert from my favorite bakery.

One night, he rubbed my feet so well, I can't tell you what it felt like he was doing—but you can imagine. I think when I started to purr his name, he began touching them more tenderly.

Our relationship provided me with an emotional comfort zone. My previous relationships had been rushed and negative. Usually, a man would date me for a while. Then as soon as we had sex, he would move to the next conquest. One ex-boyfriend even told me that I wasn't good enough in bed to keep a man interested.

Terrence hadn't even brought up lovemaking. I was beginning to worry because I had already fallen in love with him. Was I just a woman that he enjoyed spending time with? Was he not attracted to me or any woman in that way? The thoughts that began racing through my mind began to worry me. I didn't want to bring it up because I was afraid of the answer.

Fortunately, it was a question I didn't have to answer. One night after a date, he came inside my tiny apartment, and was about to kiss me goodnight. This time, the kiss took on a more passionate and hungry response. I couldn't tell who was moaning more—him or me.

Then, he stopped kissing me for a moment and looked deeply into my eyes.

"I think I'm falling in love with you." Then, he shook his head and looked at me again. "No, I know that I'm in love with you." Then, he placed his hand on my face and asked, "Don't you love me a little?"

I grabbed his hand and placed it over my heart. "Can't you feel it? Don't you know I'm in love with you?"

"Well, I'm glad I'm not the only one feeling that way," he said before he chuckled.

That night, he didn't go home, and he stayed for breakfast in the morning! I got up a little earlier than normal to make his favorite muffins. However, before they finished baking, he was already in the kitchen with his arms around me.

"I love feeling like this and being here with you," he said.

"I do, too," I said, smiling. "But I think you'd better get washed and ready for breakfast. Otherwise, you'll start something that will make us both late for work!"

He kissed me and then went into the bathroom. We ate breakfast without saying very much. But we kept smiling at each other. You know that stupid smile that you can't wipe off your face because you're so happy.

For a while, everything in my world was perfect. I was in love with a wonderful man who loved me, too. And we enjoyed spending time together—either going out or just staying at home. He had dinners at his condo, and he always let his friends know that I was the special woman in his life who made everything better.

And everything was perfect until I started leaving messages at his office that weren't being returned. I knew he was busy, but he'd always find time to return messages, even if it was later that night. I knew that some of the newness was wearing off, but it was beginning to make me feel uneasy.

Terrence had been working on a big project at work, and he'd been pulling long hours. Allyson, his administrative assistant, had worked late, too. But whenever, I went to the office, she never seemed friendly. I assumed it was because she was always busy.

Then one day, I got to the office earlier than planned. I overheard Allyson on the phone talking.

"She's a pig," Allyson snapped. "I'm going to seduce him, and then, I'm going to break them up. He belongs with me. I haven't worked all these years with him to watch some other woman take him away!"

Now, I began to understand the unreturned phone calls. I had no idea that Allyson wanted my man. And I don't think that he knew, either.

I walked through the door and tried to put a smile on my face.

"I'm here to see Terrence," I said.

"He's on the phone, right now. I'll buzz him when he's finished. Have a seat," she commanded.

I didn't bother to make small talk. I realized that this woman not only hated me, but also was after my man. She was beautiful and successful and worked with Terrence every day. Would I stand a chance if she really went out of her way?

Finally, Terrence came out, and we left for lunch. I was so shaken; I could barely eat. I was distracted and nervous.

"What's wrong?" Terrence asked.

"Nothing's wrong," I replied.

"I know when something is bothering you, Jasmine. What is it?" he asked, sharply.

I couldn't say what was really bothering me, that I was afraid that his assistant would go after him. So, I decided to talk to him about his late hours.

"You know I'm working on a project. What do you think I'm doing?" he inquired.

"I don't know. That's why I'm asking. You and your assistant seem pretty chummy to me. What's really going on?"

Instead of immediately pacifying my fears, he became silent. Then, his eyes slanted piercingly toward mine.

"Allyson works for me, and that's all you need to know."

I had never known Terrence to speak so sharply. He was attracted to her, I could tell. And that only meant that I would lose him. I didn't have the kind of job she did or the kind of looks she did. Even though Terrence made me feel gorgeous, I was really a Plain Jane.

Instead of responding, I just began to eat my meal quicker. I wanted this lunch to be over as soon as possible. I didn't want to hear him start to talk about his new woman. I wouldn't be able to take it. Then, I left quickly, muttering something about having to return to work.

That night, Terrence didn't call at all. I checked my e-mail to see if he sent a note, but he hadn't. I was miserable. I wanted to call him, but I knew that I shouldn't.

I tried to stay busy. Nadine had just discovered she was pregnant, so her husband had taken her on a romantic vacation. So, I couldn't hang out with her. And I really didn't feel like being with my other friends.

So, when my boss asked if I would be available to work in another office for a week, I jumped at the opportunity. It was only a few towns over, but the company was going to put me up in a hotel for the five days I was going to be there.

Maybe a different location will give me a new attitude. I don't want to spend all my time thinking about Terrence, I thought.

The office was busy, but the work wasn't difficult. I really enjoyed working with my new colleagues. I was beginning to contemplate asking for a transfer. Maybe leaving town was exactly what I needed to do. I needed to have new memories to replace all the sad ones I had of Terrence and me. We were so happy together, or at least that's what I thought.

The night I finally returned home, I was so tired that I went directly to bed. I was sleeping soundly when I heard a loud sound. It sounded as though someone were knocking on my door.

I must have been dreaming. I couldn't imagine anyone knocking at my door so late. Maybe it was an emergency. That had to be it.

I must have fallen asleep because the knock or banging on my door alerted me to my senses. I wiped my eyes hard, wondering who could be knocking as if their life depended on it. I stared at my watch. It was after one o'clock in the morning.

I opened the door and froze when I saw that it was Terrence. I was about to close the door on his face when he pushed it open and walked in, slamming it behind him. I could tell that he was furious as hell. He marched into my living room, and began pacing the floor.

"Where on earth have you been?"

"Away on business! Now, will you please just leave?"

"Not until you give me an explanation. I've been so worried, but you didn't care about that. I can't believe you wouldn't return my phone calls or e-mails. I thought you cared about me. I thought what we had was special.

"What is with you women? You're always talking about not finding a good man. But when one tries to treat you right, you throw it in his face. You're no better than Allyson!"

"Allyson. I'm not at all like Allyson, that witch!"

"Yes, you are! Allyson and I started going out when I first started at the company. I thought she really liked me, but she just wanted me because she thought I would be climbing the corporate ladder. She wanted to be seen on my arm, but she didn't really care for me. I vowed never to get involved with another woman like that. I thought you were different; I thought you really loved me.

"And the worst part is, Allyson was the one telling me all along that you were fooling me. She even came on to me a few times, and I always pushed her aside. I told her that I had found the woman I was going to spend the rest of my life with."

"Wait a minute. You don't want to be with Allyson. You want to be with me?" I asked.

"Yes! But I know you don't want me."

"Of course, I want you. I love you, Terrence. I thought you wanted to be with Allyson."

Then, I asked him to sit down, and I explained what I had overhead in his office. And I told him that I thought he didn't want me any longer, and that I had worked in another office.

We talked for a long time that night. We talked about our hopes and desires for the future. And we committed to exploring a future together.

Terrence didn't propose that night, but I believed he would. After that night, the time we spent together seemed better. Although we had been close for a while, the time we shared seemed more intimate.

One night at dinner, Terrence began talking about how much he loved me.

"Jasmine, you're beautiful inside and outside. My life was just plain and boring before you came into it."

"Oh, Terrence. I feel exactly the same way."

Then, he reached over and grasped my hand.

"Jasmine, I can't imagine getting old without you. I can't imagine anyone else being the mother of my children. I just can't imagine living without you."

Then, he let go of my hand and reached into his pocket. He pulled out a box and smiled. "Will you marry me, Jasmine, and make me the happiest man in the world?"

"Yes. Oh, yes."

We kissed and some of the other patrons began clapping.

That was six months ago. Neither Terrence nor I wanted to want any longer than that. But I told him I would need at least six months to plan a wedding.

We had decided to get married in the park. And the day was beautiful. Part of me still couldn't believe that I was marrying the man of my dreams.

"Hurry up, Jasmine," Nadine said. "You don't want to keep the man waiting."

"No, I don't," I replied. "I can't wait to get started on our life together."

It has been three months since that wonderful day. It's still hard for me to believe I'm married, but I'm glad I found my true love!

THE END

CHEAPSKATE
WEDDING GUEST
A bride tells all

"This is odd," I said.

"What?"

"Did we receive a wedding gift from Uma?"

"Hold on. Let me check." My husband rifled among the assortment of white and silver gift bags. "Not that I can see. Why?"

"I'm writing our thank-you notes, and I want to mention how much we will enjoy using whatever thingy it is that we will end up returning, and I can't fill in the blank unless I know what Uma got us."

Hal laughed. "Rita, maybe she mailed it to us after the wedding and it got lost. It's only been two days since we got back from our honeymoon."

I sighed. How could I forget our perfect honeymoon? "I wish we could go back to the islands and not worry about these mundane details."

My husband put his arms around me. "Honey, writing a thank-you note or even sixty-five isn't going to kill us. Think of all the fun you'll have returning everything."

"You're right. I'll mail the other thank-you notes. We'll give Uma a week to redeem herself."

My husband rolled his eyes at me.

One week later, I checked the mail, still no gift from Uma. I was delighted to see, however, that our wedding pictures had arrived, so when Hal got home from work, we savored them. We relived so many moments, I could almost hear the classical guitarist, smell the glorious bouquet of roses and lilies, and taste the champagne. I was glowing with memories, until I spotted the picture of Uma.

"Would you look at this?" I said. "Uma certainly is enjoying her prime rib."

Hal examined the picture. "That was some good eating."

"I'm referring to the fact that she clearly chowed down, but failed to leave a gift," I said.

"Still no gift, huh?"

"No, and unlike you, I'm getting more upset by the day."

Hal answered me with a frown.

"And here's a picture of her goofball date spilling a bottle of expensive champagne over his shiny head," I said.

I pulled the two pictures out and posted them on the refrigerator.

Hal watched me with a bewildered look. "Why on earth are you doing that? To torture yourself?"

"No, to remind myself that something needs to be done about Uma's transgression."

"Rita, it's one gift. She's the only one who didn't bring one. Let's overlook it, shall we?"

"No, we shall not. You're a man. You don't understand. First of all, I waited until I was thirty-five years old to get married." Hal put a finger in one of his ears, which cued me that my shrieking hurt his delicate eardrums.

I gave him a wave of dismissal. "Do you have any idea how many gifts I've bought for bridal showers and baby showers? That includes Uma when she got married to what's-his-face. We all knew that wouldn't last. Did I get the gift back when he left her? No."

"If it hadn't been for what's-his-face, otherwise known as Archie, you and I may never have met," he said. "And that's more important than any gift."

"True, they set us up on that blind date three years ago." I looked up into Hal's face. "The point is that what comes around goes around, and I want what's coming to me."

Hal shrugged, plopped down in front of the television, and picked up the remote. He remained quietly engrossed in a golf tournament for a few moments.

"Maybe she doesn't know the rules. Not everyone is as sophisticated as you," he said, not taking his eyes off the screen.

Was that sarcasm I detected? "Every woman over the age of eighteen knows the rules or she has no business calling herself a woman."

"Maybe one of the caterers stole it from the gift table."

"Surely not. Why stop at one gift? No, this is definitely a blatant disregard for the mores of polite society."

Hal turned up the volume on the television.

I paced the floor of the living room, blocking Hal's view now and then, fretting over what to do next. Then, in a flash of brilliance, I snapped my fingers and practically sprinted to my desk. I burrowed through my wedding folder for the itemized reception bill and tallied up the cost of two prime rib dinners and one bottle of champagne. I almost charged her for two bottles, but I only had proof for one. I generated a bill on the computer for the amount, found duplicate pictures of Uma and baldy, and stuffed everything into an envelope addressed to Uma.

The next afternoon, after my trip to the post office, my spirits lifted. Maybe nothing would come of it, but at least Uma would understand that I was no fool. I didn't mention the bill to Hal, deciding to put the whole incident behind me.

117

Four days later, I sat waiting and worrying by the phone until midnight. Hal hadn't come home from work.

When the phone finally rang, it was two o'clock in the morning. I snatched up the receiver.

"Rita, this is Uma." Great.

"I guess you opened your mail."

"Yes."

"Feeling a bit awkward?"

"Not really."

"Why's that?" I asked.

"I was waiting for a thank-you note from you, because as you recall, I provided the best gift of all—the husband. Had I not introduced you to Hal, there wouldn't have been a wedding."

I was stunned. "That's insane, Uma."

"Really? I don't think it's any more insane than sending me a bill for my food and drink at the reception. But, dear, the bill is the least of your worries. I'm calling to let you know that you won't need to send me a thank-you note for providing the groom after all."

"What are you talking about?"

"I called Hal when I received your bill. In disbelief, he came over to see it with his own eyes, and well, let's just say, my gift to you has been returned to me. Unlike you, I think I can actually appreciate him."

THE END

118

THE WEDDING DRESS
Who would have thought that $45 spent at a thrift store could make so many young women so happy?

"**I** have to drop off some rolls for my mother at the thrift shop," Cassie said.

And that's how it started.

Her mother was a volunteer at the local thrift shop and Cassie and I were on our way to the mall to shop for my wedding dress. Or to look. Cassie and I went way back—high school friends since the day she got dumped by her first boyfriend in tenth grade and I told her to send him a drop-dead card and she and I became friends because I, too, had recently been dumped. Well, not exactly dumped; I wasn't really serious about that creep, Glenn, but in eleventh grade you have to start thinking of the prom, right?

History. All in the past now that I was engaged to Clay and planning a wedding, although it would be a very small affair.

Cassie and I shared a small apartment near the mall. She worked as a receptionist at the hospital and I was with a law firm—not a paralegal; I did all the grunt work like phones and messages and appointments. I liked it well enough but ever since I was knee-high to a grasshopper I wanted to be married, like Barbie and Ken. I know that puts me up on the shelf for good, but I suppose I wanted what my parents had—a good, solid marriage, a nice home, three kids, and a mortgage, so to speak.

Meeting Clay was like my guardian angel had heard my prayers. My dates until then had been mostly guys who were either broke, only wanted to go to bed with me, or just were not interested in a long-term relationship. Like one of them said: "Honey, like the bees, I like to sample all the honey before I commit to one flower."

He lasted for three dates. And then I met Clay—a tall, athletic guy with a shock of sandy-blond hair and a cute way of squinting his blue eyes and stammering whenever he got a little shy. I found that endearing the first time he asked me for a date.

"If you—if you want, that is—I mean, like—maybe we could have dinner?"

When I told Cassie about him she laughed. "At least he won't try to get you into bed on the first date. By the time he comes around to asking it'll be too late!"

We laughed then, but soon I realized that Clay was just a little shy

119

sometimes. Maybe it was a little odd for a twenty-one-year-old guy, but he explained it to me later. He'd been shy since childhood and in a family with three older sisters, he'd learned early on that it was easiest to be the quiet one. My kind of guy.

Clay and I had been dating for about four months when it happened. I was mugged in the parking lot of our building because I stayed late at the office and that dark winter night, the guy saw me and grabbed me, tried to tear my purse from my arm, and then threw me down onto the concrete. I hit my head, hard. I must've been knocked out for a second or two.

Clay was driving out of the lot when he saw this happen, stopped his car, and leaped out to try to nab the guy, who saw him and fled. Clay rushed to my side and picked me up and he insisted on taking me to the hospital because I was kind of out of it.

As it turned out, I had a mild concussion, the creep had stolen my purse, and I was laid up for a few days. Clay came around with a bag of apples, of all things, and he and Cassie took good care of me.

"Keep him; he'll last," Cassie sagely advised.

And he did.

I took him home to meet my parents and they liked him and then one day, we got engaged. No drum roll or fanfare—Clay just pulled out a ring. Okay, so it isn't as big as any of Elizabeth Taylor's gems, but it's beautiful just the same.

"Should we get married?" he asked me.

Should we. I loved it. Of course we should! As it was, we'd been sort of like part-time lovers, whenever Cassie made herself scarce and we had the apartment to ourselves. I'd already found out something about myself: I am a cuddler. I love to cuddle and hold hands as much as I like sex. And so does Clay. We would lie in my bed together, quietly holding each other with sex like a gift to come, and we would just be so incredibly happy. Is that why my parents have a good marriage? Is there some kind of cosmic communication that engenders when two people just hold each other and become like the proverbial one?

All I know is that I wanted to marry Clay. And I wanted a wedding. No, I wanted a wedding dress—something I could keep packed away in a box with black tissue paper so it would not yellow with age and take it out one day for a daughter and maybe even a daughter-in-law to wear.

Sentimental?

We're out there; some of us just keep it to ourselves.

My parents were happy for me, for us. And they went along with our idea of a small wedding reception at home. My father, an insurance salesman, is by no means wealthy; still, he would've given me a bigger wedding, but Clay and I actually preferred a small wedding.

Anyway, we set a date—early June, so the reception could be held at the house and spill out into the back garden. I started buying bridal magazines and Cassie and I looked at all kinds of wedding dresses. And I have to say that when we started poking around in bridal shops—

I got the shock of my young life.

"Eight hundred dollars?" I said to a woman in one of those shops. "For one dress?"

You can see where I come from. I love clothes, but I don't look for name brands—just sales. I suppose in that way I'm like any other working girl. Ralph Lauren? Sure—if it's an end-of-the-season sale and fifty percent off. I mainly wear pants and either tops or sweaters to work, depending on the weather.

On the day in question, Cassie and I were going to browse around our one big mall in town, The Crossing. It's anchored by two name department stores and in between there are a lot of shops and one bridal shop.

We parked at the thrift and went in. Cassie's mother, a petite, dyed blonde, kissed Cassie and hugged me.

"Where are you two off to?" she asked brightly.

Cassie grinned. "What else? Malling."

"Listen, hon, your Uncle Phil—that birthday thing. . . ."

Mrs. Wheeler began to talk to Cassie so I kind of wandered off and started browsing the racks. Thrift shops are fun, if you've never been in one. They don't just sell clothes; they sell knickknacks and furniture and jewelry and lots of books and shoes—a real smorgasbord of things.

And then I saw it:

A wedding dress.

On a pretty, brunette mannequin; pale ivory silk with a beaded bodice, tiny little pearls that encircled a sweetheart neckline. It was cut princess style with the skirt flaring out a bit at the bottom, hinting at a train.

I stared at the dress and wondered where it had come from. Who would donate their wedding dress to a thrift shop? Especially this one; my by-now trained eye could see that it had most certainly not come off the bargain rack in Filene's Basement. I was staring and wondering whom the bride could be when Cassie's mother came up to me and put her arm around me.

"Isn't it lovely?" she gushed. "Just right for you."

"Me?" I said, and felt a frisson of excitement that made me feel all trembly.

"Mom, who in the world would drop off their wedding dress at a thrift shop?" Cassie asked, coming over to where we stood.

Mrs. Wheeler shrugged. "Oh, I don't know, honey—I wasn't here when it came in. Evelyn handles all the merchandise . . . and this one is a real prize. I don't even think we should sell it; we should just keep it here for show."

"What are you asking for it?" Cassie asked.

"Let me look." Mrs. Wheeler hunted around the back of the mannequin and found the price tag. "Here it is: forty-five dollars. Oh, my! What a bargain, huh, girls?"

Forty-five dollars.

I stared at the dress and like I said—it's like it was talking to me, needing me, wanting me.

I'm a touchy-feely kind of person. Tentatively, I reached out and felt the hem. And paused.

"There's a, um . . . a stain," I said.

Mrs. Wheeler peered at where I pointed and nodded. "Oh, yes—so there is! Looks like coffee, I'm afraid—not a big stain; apparently it wasn't noticed right away and the cleaner couldn't get it out. Not a big stain, though—no larger than a nickel, I would say. . . ."

And it wasn't a bad stain, by any means. One could easily miss it and when the dress moved, I decided, it wouldn't be noticed at all.

"Well, come on—let's get going before sundown," Cassie said to me.

Reluctantly, I followed her out of the thrift shop. We'd only gone a few blocks when I said to her: "Turn around. Let's go back."

She stared at me quizzically. "Back where? Did you leave your purse?"

I shook my head. "No. I want to buy that wedding dress."

"You what? It's used, Bailey—in a thrift shop, for Pete's sake! Are you out of your mind?"

I shook my head again. "No, I love it. I want it."

"If it's the money—I mean, if you can't afford—"

"It's not the money. I want that dress."

So Cassie turned the car around and we went back to the thrift and I was afraid someone else would've bought it but of course, not too many brides go looking for their wedding dresses in thrift shops.

Cassie's mother was surprised to see us again. "Forget something?" she asked.

Cassie rolled her eyes, gesturing with her thumb at me. "Her brain cells. Bailey wants to buy that wedding dress."

"You want to buy it, Bailey? For yourself?" Cassie's mother asked.

I nodded emphatically. "Yes. I want it." The more I thought about it, the more I knew I just had to have it.

"It may not fit. . . ." Cassie hedged.

"Well, she can try it on . . . we have a dressing room. But, honey, now—are you sure about this?" Mrs. Wheeler asked, her voice and face filled with concern as she sweetly patted my arm. "I mean, well . . . it's used, dear."

"I know. I don't mind that. Anyway, I can try it on, can't I?"

"Oh, of course, honey. Cassie, just help me get it off the mannequin. . . ."

Soon I was in a very small, cramped, little room at the back of the thrift, taking off my pants and T-shirt and with Cassie and her mother's help, feeling the soft silk of the wedding dress fall slowly down over my shoulders, down to my toes. Then I was staring into a not-too-clear mirror at my reflection.

I had a sudden feeling of both sadness and elation. I mean it was like I'd run a race and come to the finish line; the dress was me, it was mine—it hugged me, talked to me—needed me.

"Darn. It fits," Cassie said even as she buttoned the last, tiny, delicate, silk-covered button up the back.

"Had to cost over five hundred dollars new," her mother mused, standing at the open door of the dressing room, looking at me.

And soon Evelyn, the manager of the shop, and a couple of other customers were peering in over the women's shoulders and oohing and ahhing at me in my finery.

"I must admit, Bailey—you look gorgeous in it," Cassie said.

Her mother nodded earnestly, looking at me with tears shimmering in her blue eyes. "Absolutely breathtaking, dear."

"Stunning!" a woman behind Cassie called out. "I hope you snag a man with it, darlin'!"

I already have a man, I wanted to tell her, but I was too enthralled with my image in the mirror. I wondered for a second if another bride had stared at herself in the mirror the way I was. And was she happy? Eager? Beautiful? Who was she—and where was she now?

"I'll take it," I said.

And that was that.

A little while later Cassie and I walked out of the shop with the wedding dress on a hanger. They didn't have a box big enough to pack it in and I didn't care; I had my wedding dress.

"Home," I said to Cassie. "I don't want to leave this dress in the car at the mall."

She snorted. "Who'd steal it?"

We drove to my mother's house because our apartment was small and anyway, I'd be getting married from there and, yes—I wanted my mother to see my wedding dress. She was home; she and Dad planned to go out later for dinner and she was happy to see me and my wedding dress.

"Oh, honey—you bought your dress!" she cried when she saw me carrying it into the house. "Oh, Bailey—oh, let me see it, honey! Quick!"

"Yeah—and tell her where you bought it," Cassie said with a smirk.

I took off the wrapping and held up the dress for inspection. My mother loved it—I could just tell. She caressed the delicate fabric, the seed pearls—and got all teary.

"My baby is getting married!" she wailed, and hugged me tight. "Oh, sweetheart, I hope it didn't cost you a fortune, but your dad and I will certainly help!"

Cassie laughed. "How does forty-five dollars hit you?"

"Stop that!" I scolded. "Mom, sit down. I have something to tell you."

"She means she bought it at the thrift shop—for forty-five bucks, Mrs. Rocha," Cassie said.

My mother gasped, put out a hand and touched the dress . . . and stared in wonder.

"She's right, Mom; that's where I bought it and I want you to like it because I do and . . . and. . . ."

I started to cry. Don't ask me why; I was just suddenly overcome with what I had done, I wanted my mother to love the dress and to tell me that it was all right and Clay . . . I wanted him to love it, too.

And my dear mother turned to me and hugged me. "Honey, if this is what you want—if it will make you happy—then I love it, Bailey. After all, it's only a dress; your happiness is what matters and if this is what you want, so be it."

Can't get better than that. I cried—we all had tears—hugged, and then I faced the other hurdle.

Poor Clay. He's just not into weddings. I was, of course, and when I told him about the dress—I didn't let him see it, of course; I'm pretty much of a traditionalist in that department, so he'd only be seeing me in it on our wedding day—he did have a few reservations.

"Bailey, if it's the money, we're okay there," he began gently.

"No, it's not the money at all. It's the dress, Clay. The minute I saw it I knew I had to have it and—" I hugged him. "—it's the best bargain we'll ever get!"

My mother took the dress to the cleaner's—she insisted—and she told me that he examined the small stain and determined with his expert eye that it looked like a food stain or a coffee stain and he would do the best he could to remove it. As if it mattered; as it was, it was hardly noticeable at the bottom of the hem and it would be less so at the reception, where I might very well spill something on it, too!

On my wedding day, it rained in the morning.

"This is good luck," my bridesmaid and cousin, Gina, confidently assured me. "Sun will shine later."

And it did. And the moment I walked down the aisle to Clay in my thrift shop wedding dress, it was like there were drum rolls and music and fanfare and laughter and love. Clay's eyes shone with love and pride as he took me for his bride. And, yes, later, in the garden, I did get a few stains on the hem because of the rain and I felt that was good luck, too!

Clay and I went to Las Vegas for our honeymoon—an overnight trip because we didn't want to spend too much money. Clay and I both wanted to buy a house as soon as possible so we wouldn't waste any more of our hard-earned money on rent than necessary, so we were saving every penny we could. For the time being I left my wedding dress at my parents' house, safely packed away in black tissue paper in this huge box in the attic.

I liked being married. I liked being a Mrs., and not a Miss or a Ms.. I know that sounds strange to some, but to me, it meant I belonged and that is what I loved about it. Like the Bible says, two by two into Noah's ark. There must be something to that.

Anyway, shortly after our wedding my parents got an offer on their house that they simply couldn't refuse. The real estate market was booming in our area, they'd lived in our house for over twenty-five years, and they didn't have children at home anymore so they decided they didn't need the house anymore.

"We've looked at the condos over by the lake—over in the Emerald Glade development," Mom told me. "We can get a good-sized two-bedroom, bath-and-a-half for a great price and there'll be no more lawn mowing or basement flooding or roof leaking!" She laughed when she said that.

"Hold on," I told her. "Clay and I are looking forward to owning our own home—and all that goes with it!"

She chuckled. "Good. You have our blessings. Meanwhile, I'm going to sell most of the furniture in the house; we won't need all of it, so come get what you want."

Actually, there wasn't much that I wanted. My parents have never really gone in for antiques, and most of the furniture was from the year One. I told my mom and she laughed.

"Go up into the attic," she said. "I've saved stuff from when you were in kindergarten; you might want some of it for your children someday."

Don't most mothers save things like that? There were stuffed animals and Barbies galore and my dollhouse that Dad made for me and even the bit of patchwork quilt I'd stitched way back when I thought—for about a month—that I might become a designer.

I went over to Mom and Dad's with Clay one Saturday and we went up into the attic and I began to tear into some crates and an old chest and then—there it was:

My wedding dress, still in the long, gray box the cleaner had packed it in.

Tenderly, I showed it to Clay. "Remember this? My wedding dress."

He smiled. "Yeah. That . . . it won't fit in our closet back at the apartment," he said, his eyes meeting mine.

I nodded, lovingly stroking the box. "I'll make it fit. I can't give this up," I said. "One day, we'll have our own house and I'll be glad I kept it."

"You were one pretty sight, coming down that aisle," Clay said, and for a guy who's not too demonstrative, he grabbed me and right there in my parents' attic with Mom and Dad downstairs in the kitchen, we made love standing up.

Do you still wonder why I like being married?

Love is like soft rain. It washes over you at unexpected times and refreshes and rejuvenates.

I took the wedding dress to our apartment.

And then it started.

I couldn't fit the huge box in any of our three small closets so I shoved it under our bed. When Clay and I got married and I moved into his apartment he got rid of his double bed and we bought a queen-sized bed that's set high up from the floor. I guess I like to feel like a queen or something in that bed, but the good thing about it is that the box fit under it, a bit snug but safe.

About two weeks later it started. I really didn't give the box with the dress in it much thought but then one night, I had this dream that was so real, I woke up in a sweat and shaking and Clay heard me and woke up, too.

He pulled me close. "Hey, Bailey, take it easy—it was just a bad dream."

"Yeah . . . I guess, but . . . it was so real." I was shaking, drenched in sweat. "I saw her . . . she was so real, standing over there by the door. . . ."

"Who? You saw someone in your dream?"

I nodded. "My wedding dress . . . a young woman was wearing it . . . she was so real. . . ."

"Honey, it was just a dream," Clay soothed, kissing my damp forehead. "Just close your eyes and go back to sleep."

I tried. But the dream clung to me in the morning and when I went to work I called Cassie to tell her about it. She laughed at me.

"Listen, girly—you have a thing about that dress. Forget it, married lady. Anyway, what about Saturday? Want to mall it or will you be spending the day in bed with you-know-who?"

"You're jealous," I teased. "What about what's-his-name?"

Cassie had changed jobs recently; she'd gotten a job working in the municipal building in the tax department and had been bragging about a guy she worked with. He was divorced, no kids, and he'd asked her out for coffee.

"I'm working on him," Cassie said. "Let me know about Saturday but if I get a better offer—forget it!"

I did meet Cassie for a couple of hours on Saturday and she went on and on and on about Stephen, the new guy in her life.

"He's kind of gun-shy, I guess, but I'm working on him."

"You can borrow my wedding dress anytime," I told her.

She winked and smiled devilishly. "Keep it handy."

Not long afterward, I had the dream again. Only that time, the girl in the wedding dress seemed so sad, like she'd been crying. Again, I woke up in a sweat. Again, Clay held me and soothed me. I began to think I was losing my marbles. For some reason, the dress has clearly become an obsession for me. And how could I avoid thinking about it when it was right there in the box under my bed?

My mother had a garage sale and I went to help her—so did Clay. It was a mild fall day and people came in droves. I've never seen people so anxious to buy "stuff"—that's what Clay calls it. Mom sold some pieces of furniture—chairs and a card table—and lots of kitchen things.

"Remember: If you see anything you want, just put it aside," she told me.

Then Mr. Dimanto arrived in a van with two of his sons. Gus Dimanto owns the Italian restaurant in town, Bella Luna. I was surprised to see him. I've known him for like, forever; my parents often took us to eat at Bella Luna when we were growing up and it's a great restaurant for a date, too, oddly enough. Anyway, Mr. Dimanto greeted me effusively and then turned to my mother.

"I brought my boys, Marie. I hope it fits in the van," he said.

"We can try," Mom said, and led him and his boys into the house.

Of course I followed, intrigued, wondering what my mother had sold him. But once we were in our dining room, I immediately knew what it was. A long time ago my parents bought this old sideboard—six feet long with lots of drawers and a couple of cubbyholes—from The Salvation Army. My father refinished it and all while I was growing up it took up a good part of our dining room, but we all loved it—it was like a part of the family, really. Now, though, apparently Mom was selling it because of course, it was too big for the condo and I had little use for it in our apartment. Even if we bought a house one day, it's really not my style.

And yet, as they carried it out of the house, I felt a twinge. Like I was seeing an old friend leave forever.

"I kind of hate to see it go," I said to my mother.

"Things," she said, shrugging her shoulders. "Things are . . . just things. Never love something that can't love you back, Bailey," she said.

Never love something that can't love you back.

Her words echoed in my head for days. And they began to make so much sense when I kept having what I called "the dream."

It was always the same: The girl would come dressed in my—our—wedding dress and she would look so sad. And I would wake up crying or, because I did not want to worry Clay, I'd keep the dream to myself. But it never left me; it was like an albatross around my neck. I began to wonder if the dress was haunted or bad luck or what?

But that was nonsense. After all, Clay and I were doing just fine. We were incredibly happy together, saving our money, and on weekends, we were doing what real estate people hate: We were house looking. Not house buying, mind you—just house looking. It was fun; we were always on the lookout for Open House signs and we'd walk in and pretend we were very interested in buying, and then we'd go home and Clay and I would go over the figures and we'd know it was going to be a while before we could afford a down payment at the exorbitant prices of the day.

Then one Saturday night after my parents had moved into their condo, we all met at Bella Luna for dinner. We were greeted with hugs from Gus Dimanto, of course, and then Mom and I went to stand by "our" sideboard, now a showpiece in the restaurant with a display of flowers and some rustic Italian pottery on top.

"She sure is happy here," Mom remarked, smiling as she ran her hand tenderly over the polished wood. "You know, Bailey, I told you that things are just things . . . but I wonder if sometimes, they have a kind of . . . personality. . . ." She chuckled, shaking her pretty, dark head. "Oh, just listen to me! What a foolish idea! Anyway, let's eat!"

Her words stayed with me then and when I had the dream again. I knew she was right; never love anything that can't love you back. But I was doing just that with the wedding dress. And maybe the girl who'd given it to the thrift shop was doing it, too, for by then, I was sure she was the "ghost" of the bride who'd worn the dress who kept appearing in my dream. Or the spirit of the girl who'd given it up. I had no answers. All I knew was that I had to be rid of the dream to get on with my life.

Cassie's responsible for what happened next. Or was it my angels who took over for me? You see, I believe in angels. I believe they watch over us and guide us, if and when we let them. Mom's stories

128

to us kids when we were very young made a real impression on me. I began to think that the wedding dress and I shared some kind of special "relationship," but that it was time to let it go.

I was having lunch with Cassie one day when she told me this story:

"You know I work in the municipal building and the other day, I was talking to this woman who's an aide to a judge and she told me that a young couple had come in to get married and the girl wore jeans—new and clean, mind you, but jeans just the same—and she confided to the woman that she wished she could've been married in a wedding dress, but they didn't have any money and their families didn't approve of the marriage."

I had tears in my eyes by the time she finished the story.

"That is so sad," I said. "I know how she felt; most girls want a wedding dress."

"At least the first time!" Cassie laughed.

I hoped that girl would be happy in her marriage, even without a wedding dress for her memory book. And when I told Clay about her, he, too, was touched by the story.

"I guess we can't have everything we want in life," he said.

And then I did a silly thing.

I stopped in at the thrift shop one afternoon on my lunch hour and asked if Evelyn was in. Evelyn is the manager. First I looked around and did not see a wedding dress on display; Evelyn was in a back room filled to the ceiling, almost, with donated clothing. When a salesgirl led me back there, Evelyn was up to her knees in secondhand clothing.

"Hi! I hope you're here to volunteer!" she kidded. "Every once in a while people clean out closets or someone dies and the heirs bundle up all the unwanted stuff and donate it . . . say, didn't you. . . ?"

I nodded, smiling. "Yes, I did. I bought the wedding dress a while ago."

She nodded, curious. "I remember that. We generally don't do much business in wedding dresses; girls usually want to keep them forever in an attic."

Like me, I wanted to tell her. In a box under my bed and haunting my dreams. But I didn't say that to that kind and busy woman.

"I don't suppose you know or remember who donated the dress, do you?" I asked carefully.

She shook her head. "Oh, my, no. I'm not the only one receiving, you know; the front desk takes in donations, too." She studied me curiously for a moment, cocking her head to one side. "Why do you ask?"

"Oh, just curious," I said. I was not about to tell her that the dress had become an obsession with me. And Mom's words kept ringing in my ears: Don't love anything that can't love you back.

I left the thrift shop after buying two lovely scarves—a dollar each—and felt very virtuous about it. And when I showed them to Clay and told him how much they cost, he laughed.

"Maybe we ought to buy all our clothes at the thrift. That way, we can afford a house in ten years!"

But I already knew what I wanted to do: I wanted to donate the dress—my forty-five-dollar, secondhand wedding dress—to some other young woman who wanted to be a bride in all her finery. It's Cassie who gave me the idea when she told me about the girl who got married in jeans, but who longed to be a blushing bride in a fairytale wedding dress.

I didn't tell Cassie or Clay or my mother or anyone about my idea.

As it was, I often drove by this small church—the denomination is not important—located in a neighborhood of run-down houses and a couple of two-story apartment buildings. Franklintown, it was called—filled with working-class people, but a neighborhood that was clean and looked like a homey place to live, just the same.

One day I visited the rectory next door to the church, a small, faded, brick, ranch-style house, and I met the minister and his wife. I told them why I was there.

"I want to give you my wedding dress to keep here for any bride to wear if she can't afford one but wants to wear one. It won't fit everyone, of course, and maybe brides mostly want their own wedding dresses. . . . I'll be frank with you; I bought it at a thrift shop—it was my own wedding dress on my wedding day and I've been so very, very happy with my husband ever since. It's a good, fine dress, you see. It ought to be used—not saved away in a box in a dusty attic. . . ." I blushed at their curious, bemused smiles. "Am I making any sense?"

I was babbling and afraid I'd start to cry. The minister's wife saw this and reached out to hug me.

"I think that is the most generous idea I have ever heard. Yes, yes, we'll take it. And we'll let our people know, and I'm sure some of our brides will be happy to borrow it, use it, walk down the aisle in it . . . what a lovely thing to do!"

A few days later I took the wedding dress to the church, handed it to the minister, and received his blessing. I was a bit sorry to give away the dress, and yet, I felt a frisson of relief and happiness when I did just that. After all, I had my memories and my wedding photos, and I liked to think of some other bride or brides who might wear the dress one day and look lovely, feel lovely, and fulfill all of the hopes, wishes, and dreams wrapped up in that lovely, lovely wedding dress.

Clay was stunned when I told him what I'd done. "Why didn't you tell me?" he asked.

130

I took his hands in mine. "I needed to do it by myself, honey," I told him. "I loved the dress, but that's all it is—just a dress—just a thing. It can't love me back." I kissed him tenderly. "I have you for that."

"I'll buy you a silver wedding dress on our twenty-fifth anniversary," he said, pulling me into his arms . . . where I intend to stay forever.

And oh, yes—the dreams—or nightmares, if you want to call them that—stopped that very night.

I think she—the first bride—approves.

THE END

www.ingramcontent.com/pod-product-compliance
Lightning Source LLC
Chambersburg PA
CBHW071354170626
46811CB00003B/1129